# THE SEARCH FOR
## Happily-Ever-After

# THE SEARCH FOR
## Happily-Ever-After

* by Patricia Baehr *

Illustrations by Randel J. Chavez

BridgeWater Books

*For Gemma*

Published by BridgeWater Books,
an imprint of Troll Associates, Inc.

Designed by Aileen Friedman.

Printed in the United States of America.

10  9  8  7  6  5  4  3  2  1

*Library of Congress Cataloging-in-Publication Data*
Baehr, Patricia Goehner.
The search for happily-ever-after / by Patricia Goehner Baehr.
p.  cm.
Summary: Tired of not measuring up to her sisters, Ketti finds herself
transported through a wormhole to a land of fairy-tale characters where she
helps Cinderella's coachman-rat achieve his "happily-ever-after."
ISBN 0-8167-3658-8
[1. Magic—Fiction.   2. Characters and characteristics in literature—
Fiction.   3. Sisters—Fiction.   4. Sibling rivalry—Fiction.]   I. Title.
PZ7.B1387Pu   1995   [Fic]—dc20      94-37415

# ✳ CONTENTS ✳

# ✳ CHAPTER 1 ✳

# The Rat in the Woodpile

"HOME free all!"

The game of hide-and-seek was over and so was Ketti Watson's chance of winning. Now she was going to have to show herself and let her sisters discover she had gone out of bounds. Even worse, Miranda and Ellen would know Ketti had gone onto the Kramer property, something all three of the Watson children were forbidden to do.

"Drat," Ketti said as Miranda's call came again.

"Home free all!"

It was faint. It had to travel out of the Watson back-yard, over the chest-high weeds of the neglected Kramer field, and through the logs of a rotting woodpile to reach Ketti.

"Home free all!" Ellen echoed.

Ketti stubbornly remained in the square of

powdery dirt between the woodpile and the tumble-down Kramer barn, dreading the lecture her mother would give her when she found out where Ketti had been. For Miranda and Ellen would tattle—oh, they would definitely tattle—and Ketti would probably lose dessert for a week.

"Double drat!" Ketti said more loudly when she remembered there was going to be ice cream after dinner.

"Pray, what does it portend, this doubled drat?" asked a voice.

Ketti started. Someone else was hiding outside the barn.

"Behold, it is a pleasantly warm day, is it not?" the voice pressed when she didn't answer.

"Warm enough for September," Ketti answered carefully. Did the voice belong to a boy? Could it be that awful Dennis Rafferty from down the street? Thinking she might be able to figure out his hiding place if he spoke again, Ketti kept talking. "Who wants it warm anyway when you have to spend the day in school?"

"You go to school, do you?" the voice asked. It was an odd one, not really like Dennis's at all. This voice had an accent. And there was a nasal quality to it. Of course, Dennis might be pinching his nose shut.

"Is school the custom here, Humphrey?"

Humphrey! The game had gone far enough. "I know where you are!" Ketti said. "Stop teasing or I'll . . . I'll stuff your shirt with burrs!"

Ketti stomped to the opposite side of the stacked

logs, where she expected to see stocky, fair-haired Dennis. Instead she saw a small, dark something dart into the woodpile.

Was Dennis playing a trick on her? Had he run off into the weeds, scaring up a rabbit or mouse or, or . . . Ketti ran her fingers through her hair, rejecting the thought that had popped into her head. Small, shadowy things did not speak.

"Say something again," she demanded. But there was no answer, just a soft noise from her own back-yard: Miranda and Ellen calling.

Ketti dropped down and crept back to the other side of the woodpile so she could not be seen, grumbling as she went. "Call me Humphrey, will you?"

"Is Humphrey Awl not your name?" the voice promptly asked. It came from somewhere close to Ketti. It seemed to emanate from the very bottom of the woodpile itself. "I heard them," the voice went on. "They called, 'Humphrey Awl! Humphrey Awl!' I assumed it to be you."

Imagining something like a walkie-talkie hidden in the woodpile, Ketti began to search for an antenna or some other kind of proof.

"Is everything all right?" the voice asked.

Ketti spoke as haughtily as she could. "I know what you're up to."

"Good," the voice replied. "Although I was ready to trust the tree, I was unsure. You are not what I expected. Still, you must be the right one. I mean, here I am and here you are."

With that odd pronouncement, the small, shadowy thing crept forward into the sunshine. It was a rat, a glossy black rat with large ears, round eyes, and a long, scaly tail. As Ketti stepped back, it turned a pointed muzzle to face her.

"You . . . you didn't say anything, did you?" she asked, unbelieving.

The rat tilted his head to one side and seemed to frown. "Of course I did. Does my tail seem crooked to you? I pray I have not bent my whiskers in the wormhole. They are my pride, you see. Also my curse."

Stunned, Ketti could only repeat dully, "Wormhole?"

"It is a method of travel that is most jarring to the body," the rat said. He scrambled to the top of the woodpile in a crooked line, avoiding one section of the stack. "Have you on your person, Humphrey, a bit of soap or, perchance, an inch of candle?"

Ketti shook her head. Then, understanding that the rat had misunderstood her sisters' calls of "home free all," she said, "I'm not Humphrey Awl. My name is Ketti Watson."

"Well, have you some rope, Ketti Watson?"

Switching to a nod, Ketti rooted through a pocket in her jeans to find a length of bakery twine. She'd been meaning to weave some kind of spooky, spiderwebby trap one night to scare Miranda and Ellen. But scaring Miranda and Ellen was nothing compared to a talking rat.

"How did you learn to talk?" she asked, plucking

up enough courage to dangle the string near the rat's two pairs of sharp front teeth.

Once he had grabbed the string away from her, the rat began munching eagerly. "Didn't."

"Were you born this way?"

"Nay."

"Then how did you start talking?"

Nearly four inches of the string were gone. When the rat lowered the frayed end and stared at it fondly, Ketti cleared her throat to remind him of the question.

"Indeed," he said, returning to his meal and speaking between bites and swallows. "It happened . . . all at once . . . in a bright flash of . . . of blue light."

"You were hit by lightning? I never knew lightning could make animals talk."

"It cannot—leastwise, not that I have ever heard."

Ketti snatched the twine from the rat's paws and put it behind her back. "I want to know why you talk and where you came from. No string until you tell me everything."

"Everything?"

When Ketti nodded, the rat settled himself on the woodpile with a sigh.

"To start I shall have to tell you of a time when a famine lay over the land and I often had not so much as a crumb of bread to eat, a time when I learned to content myself by eating odd bits of things I found in the cottages: soap, wax, rope . . ." The rat paused, trying, without success, to see the string behind Ketti.

"One night," he went on, "when I had traveled far

and wide in search of my dinner, I discovered a piece of goat cheese laid inside a rattrap. For a good part of the evening I struggled with the problem: How could I get the cheese without getting caught? But before I had come to any decision, I saw two other rats approaching. Thinking only that they were going to get my cheese, I rushed at the trap as they did. We were all captured. Perhaps you have heard the rest. The girl and her godmother came. They picked me." The rat lifted his head cockily. "'Most handsome whiskers,' they said. Picked me because I had the most handsome whiskers."

"Perfectly beautiful whiskers," Ketti agreed. "Picked you for what?"

"As coachman, of course. When I was coachman I wore a most distinguished mustache. But then came the lie. The godmother proclaimed everyone would live happily ever after. Was there a happily-ever-after for me? No! I can tell you, it was a great disappointment after the ball, when we all ended up on the cobblestones: a ragged girl holding one glass slipper, six green lizards, six sweating mice, a broken pumpkin, and me. Naturally I followed the girl home. I don't know what became of the others. I left the mice struggling to regain their breath. The lizards slithered off into the night. I doubt they even noticed the transformation. They made foolish men. All they wanted to do was take off their fine clothing and lie in the sun."

Ketti spoke in an awed whisper. "Were you the rat in the Cinderella story?"

"I was. I beseech you, how could a body who has once been human be happy as a rat? How?"

"You were cheated," Ketti said, full of sympathy. "You were supposed to live happily ever after and you were cheated."

"But by paw or claw I shall get what is due me," the rat said firmly. "I will be granted my happily-ever-after and once again be a man."

Ketti sat down and looked thoughtfully at her sneakers. "You know, I always wondered about Cinderella's story. Why didn't the glass slippers disappear with all of the rest of the stuff at midnight, huh? What was the fairy godmother up to?"

The rat eyed Ketti keenly. "A very good point. It is true that she appeared with great suddenness when the prince arrived, slipper in hand. One moment she was not there and the next she was waving her wand, proclaiming, 'And you shall all live happily ever after!' Ha! All but me."

"At least you can still talk."

This was dismissed with the flick of a whisker.

"So what are you going to do now?" Ketti asked.

The rat edged forward, hunching up vulturelike on the end of one log. "It is not what I am going to do, Humphrey, not I alone."

"I . . . I told you. I'm not Humphrey," Ketti stammered when he had stretched to his full height, moving between her and the sun. "I'm—"

"Come with me!" the rat said.

Ketti had an awful feeling he might lunge at her.

She leaned back, prepared to jump up quickly. "I can't go anywhere. I have to go home."

"Come," the rat said again.

"I'm not even allowed to be here," Ketti babbled. "It's against the rules. I'll bet Miranda's already gloating. She's my sister, see, the one who's three years older. She's a mathematical genius and she never gets in trouble. Really, neither of my sisters do, only me. Ellen, the baby, she's already writing out letters and making words. My parents think everything she does is wonderful. I only came here because I wanted to be the winner for once, and now I'm going to be in trouble."

The rat's mouth twisted into something resembling a smile. "I can keep you out of trouble."

"You can?"

"Most definitely. But first you must promise to help me."

"Help you how?"

"Meet me here another time."

"That's it?" Ketti asked. "Just meet you here, I wouldn't have to go anywhere?"

"Give me your word of honor," said the rat. "Say, 'I will come again.'"

Something told Ketti she'd be wiser to get up and run home, but she asked, "When?"

"Soon. Before . . . before another sun has passed."

"Okay."

"Say it."

Ketti took a deep breath. "I'll come again."

"Then farewell for now."

"But what about keeping me out of trouble?"

The rat traced the same crooked course down the face of the woodpile, speaking to her as he went. "Go home now. There will be no trouble over the time spent here. And when you return we will see about getting you your happily-ever-after."

"My what?"

But Ketti's question went unanswered. The rat had melted into darkness.

# ✳ CHAPTER 2 ✳

## *Zap!*

Once home, Ketti had little time to think about her meeting with the rat.

"Miranda called you in a long time ago," her mother said. She was draining a pot of potatoes at the sink in the kitchen of the tiny house. "Where have you been, Ketti?"

"I know where you've been," Miranda taunted.

"Set the table, Ketti," her father ordered. He took the pot from his wife and asked Miranda to fetch him the potato masher.

"Excuse me," Miranda said as she pulled Ketti away from the utensil drawer. "I have to get the masher."

"And I have to get the silverware," Ketti answered her, pushing forward again.

"Just wait your turn," said Miranda.

"Me?" Ketti's voice went shrill. "You wait."

Mrs. Watson lifted a roast out of the oven. "Girls, I asked for help, not aggravation."

"Miranda started it—"

Mrs. Watson frowned. "I don't want to hear it, Ketti. It's bad enough that you came home late. Just do your job."

"But Mom," Ketti complained anyway, "Miranda always thinks she should get everything her way because she's the oldest and—"

Mr. Watson attacked the potatoes with the masher. The pot clattered: *ka-thunk, ka-thunk.* "Didn't you hear your mother, Ketti? She doesn't want to hear it. Understand?"

"You stand?" Ellen said as she ambled into the already crowded kitchen. At two and a half, Ellen loved to repeat what she heard, but, like the last person in a game of telephone, she often got it wrong. "Stand up, Ketti!"

"Mind your own business," Ketti scolded. "It's— hey, you've got my puppets!"

For what seemed like the millionth time Ellen was playing with Ketti's hand puppets. But this time not only was she playing with them, she was wearing them on her feet as slippers. On her right foot was a prince and on her left was a witch. "*P* for puppets!" Ellen announced.

Ketti tossed the silverware onto the table and whirled around to set her younger sister down hard on her bottom.

"Ketti hurt me!" Ellen cried. "She take my *P* for puppets!"

"Aw, Ketti," said Mr. Watson. "What's the big deal about letting the baby play with your puppets?"

"She's not playing with them, she's ruining them! Look at the dirt! And here—the seam's going to rip!"

"Daddy will buy Ellen some *P* for puppets of her own," Mr. Watson promised.

Ketti couldn't believe it. "Why should Ellen get new puppets? She's the one who's wrecking mine!"

"Enough," Mrs. Watson scolded. "Sort out this silverware so we can eat."

Sullenly, Ketti did as she was told. When she had taken her place at the table, Miranda, beside her, smiled as she unfolded her napkin and smoothed it over her thighs.

"Guess what, Ketti. During winter vacation, I'm going to visit Grandma in Florida."

"WHAT?"

Mr. Watson overlooked Ketti's outburst, calmly doling out mashed potatoes with an ice-cream scoop while he explained. "Grandma called and said she would fly Miranda down for a visit. She said she was such a great houseguest last year—"

"Why Miranda again?" Ketti demanded. "Why not me this time?"

Mrs. Watson said, "Miranda's older. We didn't think you were ready to go off on your own. Maybe next year—"

"Next year?" Ketti interrupted. "You don't know that Grandma will offer again. Or that she'll want me."

"Please, Ketti," her mother said. "Can't we have a peaceful meal for a change? Let's talk about something else."

Miranda obliged, announcing, "Ketti went onto the Kramer property."

"The Kramer property?" Mr. Watson repeated.

Ketti asked, "What kind of meat is this?" but Mr. Watson ignored the attempt to change the subject.

"Is that true, Ketti?"

"This is pork," Ketti said. "I hate pork."

"I hate pork, too," Ellen chimed in.

"No, you don't, sweetie." Mrs. Watson speared a square of meat off Ellen's plate and waved it in the air before Ellen's mouth. "Open up. You love pork!"

"I hate pork," Ellen repeated.

Mrs. Watson smiled wanly. "Next time, Ketti, keep your comments to yourself."

"Pork is good," Miranda cooed. "Look, Ellen. Miranda eats hers! Mmm."

"You haven't answered my question," Mr. Watson said to Ketti.

"What question?"

Mrs. Watson shook her head as Ellen brought a fistful of mashed potatoes to her mouth. "Ketti, you know perfectly well you're not allowed on the Kramer property. Goodness knows we don't burden you with many rules. We expect you to follow the ones we do make. That old barn could collapse with the next breeze, and there could be ticks and rats and rusty nails—"

"But I didn't go there," Ketti heard herself say.

Miranda gasped. "She's lying. I saw her!"

Only Ellen continued eating. The rest stared at Ketti. She squirmed in her seat. Here it came: no ice cream.

"See, Miranda and Ellen and I were playing hide-and-seek," she started, wanting to justify herself. "And—"

"And you cheated."

At Miranda's gloating statement, something inside Ketti blew apart. "No! I hid in the flower bed. And because Miranda didn't find me, she thinks I cheated."

"I saw you," Miranda insisted. "Ellen did, too. We saw you out in front of the Kramer barn."

"I saw you," Ellen echoed.

"Maybe you saw somebody," Ketti said rashly, "but it wasn't me."

Silence followed. After a moment, Mr. Watson picked up his glass to drink and Mrs. Watson turned to Miranda.

"I've never known Ketti to lie," she said quietly. "If she claims she wasn't by the Kramer barn, she wasn't. You and Ellen must have seen someone else. The weeds make it hard to see anything, you know. Now eat your dinner. Ice cream tonight."

As silverware scraped against plates, Ketti bowed her head. She had lied. Worse, her mother had believed her and stuck up for her.

"Use a fork, sweetie," Mrs. Watson said, picking up a napkin to wipe Ellen's fingers.

Ketti stuck three pieces of pork into her mouth at once to be done with it and felt a shiver travel up her spine: The rat had been right. She hadn't gotten into trouble. Did that mean she would now have to keep her end of the bargain?

That night, clouds covered the sky like a quilt. The air that puffed into the girls' bedroom smelled of rain and dampness. Under a rumpled sheet, Ketti tossed, unable to sleep. Finally she slid out of bed and into the hallway. To one side, in the kitchen, Mrs. Watson was bent over the checkbook. To the other, in the living room, Mr. Watson tossed matched socks into a laundry basket. When he looked up, Ketti padded in to him.

"I can't sleep."

"Thirsty, Ket? Why don't you get yourself a drink of water?"

"I'm not thirsty, " Ketti told him. "I'm just . . . thinking."

Mr. Watson folded the cuff of one of Ellen's socks over its mate. "Is there something you want to talk about?"

For a moment Ketti was tempted to admit her dinnertime lie. But then she remembered the rat's talk of happily-ever-after and changed her mind. "What are wormholes?" she said instead. "I mean the traveling kind."

Her father seemed surprised. "Wormholes? Where did you hear about them?"

"Somewhere," Ketti answered vaguely. "Can you do that, travel by wormhole?"

With the last of the socks matched, Mr. Watson moved the laundry basket from the couch to the floor. Ketti sat down beside him.

"Listen here, young lady. Is this some kind of trick to stay up late?"

She shook her head. "No. I really want to know. It's keeping me awake."

"Wormholes, huh? Well, I don't teach about them in my junior high science classes, but I do know they have something to do with physics and the general theory of relativity."

Ketti made a face. "Talk so that I can understand you."

"I'll try. Einstein—you've heard of him, right? Well, Einstein said that gravity curves space and time."

Mr. Watson reached for a newspaper on the coffee table and tore out a page. He curved it so that the top half of the paper was directly above the bottom half. From where Ketti sat, it looked like a letter *U* lying on its side. He put the page into her hands.

"Hold it like that," he said. "Keep it bent. Good. Now, suppose here, at the top of the page, is one time and place—"

"Like hundreds of years ago," Ketti supplied. "Fairy-tale time."

"—and here, at the bottom of the page," Mr. Watson went on, pointing, "is another time and place."

"Right now," Ketti said. "Where we live."

"You could get from one spot to another, if you wanted"—Mr. Watson walked his fingers along the outside of the curve—"only it would take time."

"Hundreds of years," Ketti said. "And a person wouldn't live long enough to do it."

Her father nodded. "But if there were an area of extremely high gravity, space might be warped into one of those wormholes you were asking about. You know, a tunnel."

Taking a sharpened pencil, he thrust it through both sides of the paper. "Zap! From here to there, instantly."

Ketti touched the eraser at the top of the pencil and thought about the Cinderella rat. "Zap."

Mrs. Watson had come to stand in the room's doorway. She shared a smile with her husband. "Looks like we're raising a theoretical physicist."

Ketti grinned. "I'll bet Miranda and Ellen won't be theoretical fizzy—whatever you said."

The pleased looks vanished from her parents' faces.

Mr. Watson sighed. "Don't start in, Ketti."

"Why must you always compare yourself with your sisters?" Mrs. Watson added. "You're completely different people."

Ketti's heart pounded with past hurts. "You think you don't compare us? You're always wishing I could be like them, smart and cute—"

"We don't wish anything of the kind," Mrs. Watson interrupted her. "We only want you to be yourself and to be happy."

Ketti wasn't listening. "You treat me like—"

"We treat you like Ketti," her father said. "Would you want us to treat you the way we treat Miranda or Ellen? Do you really want Ellen's early bedtime or Miranda's chore of baby-sitting?"

"You're twisting everything around," Ketti accused. "You're not talking about all the good things they get, like Miranda staying up late or Ellen getting cuddled all the time."

"And aren't there good things about being Ketti?" her mother asked.

Ketti was silenced. She could not think of one good thing about being Ketti. She wasn't as smart as Miranda or as cute as Ellen. She was never the best.

"Get some sleep," her mother said, bending to place a kiss on Ketti's forehead. "If you think, I'm sure you'll find plenty of things to feel happy about. Tomorrow morning, I'll even help you make a list."

Mr. Watson tousled Ketti's hair. "When you're unhappy, kiddo, we're unhappy. Hey, shut your windows," he added as she started down the hall. "It's going to rain."

Ketti found that the storm had already begun to blow. The slats of the shutters in the girls' shared room rattled as a cool wind whistled in. Mixing with the sound was Ellen's contented sucking on her thumb and Miranda's slow, rhythmic breathing.

Ketti lowered the window sash and moved the shutters into place. When lightning forked outside, its sharp white light flashed through the wooden slats and into Ketti's eyes. It was almost as if it reached right into her brain as well, illuminating an idea she hadn't thought before. Hadn't the rat mentioned getting Ketti her own happily-ever-after? She didn't have to settle for being third best. She could be *the* best.

In the time it took for a second bolt of lightning to zigzag across the sky, Ketti decided that the rat's promise was the answer to all her problems. She changed into a pair of jeans and a sweatshirt. Then, creeping through the darkened hallway to the kitchen, she slipped through the back door and outside.

The wind forced ragged clouds over the moon's face and turned the undersides of leaves up to a black sky. It hurried her across the darkened backyard and then plunged her into a field of weeds that rippled and lashed like a sea gone mad.

"Hello!" Ketti called when she reached the far side of the woodpile. Her voice was nearly lost in the wind. "I'm here! I've come back like I said I would! Hello!"

When the first drops of rain splattered down, the moon reappeared. With it came a noise, a scrabbling, scratching sound. Turning to the barn, Ketti saw something dark move across the roof. It raced down the shingled slope, not stopping at the edge but plunging forward, forward, straight at Ketti. For a moment it was airborne, a small, furry shape silhouetted against the moon. And then it hit her. Screaming, Ketti fell backward onto the woodpile and disappeared.

# ✳ CHAPTER 3 ✳

# *The Silver Linden Tree*

Silence. Dark. Ketti knew she was screaming but no sound escaped her throat. She struggled to fill her lungs, but either there was no air or else the awful pressure on her chest kept her from breathing. Had the rat knocked the wind out of her? No. Her head, her legs and arms, her fingers, too—all were pinned by a tremendous weight. Where was she? How long before the pressure crushed her? How long before the lack of air suffocated her? Ketti couldn't think if she'd been trapped for hours or seconds. Time had no meaning, as if she no longer existed in it.

And then she was back. With a horrible rasping sound, she pulled air into her lungs. Her heart pounded in her chest—had it stopped?—and her body jerked to regain its balance.

The storm was gone and, with it, the night. Ketti was perched on the wide limb of a tree. Clinging like a burr to the front of her sweatshirt was the rat. As sunlight blinked at them through an array of heart-shaped leaves already tinged with gold, the rat plucked his claws free and sprang at the tree's enormous trunk.

"Come along!" he called as he raced down.

Ketti's voice scraped as though she hadn't used it for a hundred years. "Where? What's going on?"

Stepping from branch to branch, testing each to be sure it would hold her weight, Ketti lost sight of the rat. When she reached the last branch and dropped to the ground, she found herself in a kind of leafy tent. The tree's lowest limbs grew down instead of up. Under the highest arch stood a four-poster bed heaped with colorful quilts. It was a wood-framed double bed, and there were animals carved on both its head- and footboards. More interesting to Ketti, though, was the person lying beneath the quilts.

"Excuse me?" Ketti called out questioningly.

She was the oldest woman Ketti had ever seen. A wispy cloud of white hair crowned her head and the skin on her face and neck hung in pleats.

"Are you awake?" Ketti asked, gently shaking the mattress. Something like straw crunched softly, but the woman didn't stir. A black bird let out a raucous cry as it flew from the tree.

"There is no sense in trying to wake her," a familiar voice said.

Ketti spun around to discover the rat creeping along the length of a low branch. Seeing him reminded her of the crushing dark, and she asked, "What did you do to me? Where have you brought me?"

"*Shh!*" the rat hissed.

His warning seemed unnecessary since the old woman remained still. Much too still, Ketti thought. "What's the matter with her?"

The rat had reached the trunk and was making his way to the ground. Like a squirrel, he held easily to the bark. "Nothing is the matter with her now. Her friends will see to her remains."

"Remains? You mean she's dead?"

"Yes, but you needn't feel sorry for her. At one hundred and twenty-six, she had lived a very full—"

"You pushed me into a wormhole," Ketti said, suddenly understanding what had happened. "I could have been killed!"

"Nonsense. Here you are, as strong as an ogre, as healthy as a hag, as fit as a fairy—"

"Where's here?" Ketti demanded.

The rat nestled himself amid the fallen leaves. "We are perhaps ten leagues southwest of Cinderella's palace and another two days south of the sleeping castle. That, by the by, is where we will be heading in order to see the last of the godmother's spells to its proper completion. When that has occurred, I shall be turned back into a man and you shall get your happily-ever-after."

Ketti forgot about the ordeal of the wormhole with

the mention of happily-ever-after. "How do you know we'll get it?"

"It was the godmother's promise to me. I went to her to complain about how she had cheated me, but alas, it was too late. She was already dying, too weak to do magic. Believe it or not, she wanted help from me!"

The rat distorted his face, imitating the fairy godmother for Ketti. "'Have pity, dearie, and be a prince,' she said. 'I'll not rest easy unless I know someone is taking care of my last spell.'"

"And you said you would," Ketti prompted.

The rat nodded. "In return, she promised me happily-ever-after. It was her suggestion that I turn to the tree for help. This tree is magic. It was the one that supplied her wands. And through the wormhole, it took me to you."

"Just how do you know about Einstein and wormholes and all that?" Ketti wanted to know.

The rat looked blank at the mention of Einstein. "It was the godmother who told me about the wormhole. Haven't you ever seen them, the little tunnels the worms make? Not all are for traveling—"

A thought popped into Ketti's head. She stood and pointed to the woman on the bed. "Is that her? Is that the godmother, Cinderella's fairy godmother?"

"And godmother to many others besides, including the one in the sleeping castle. You can always tell them by their hands," the rat said. "Fairies, I mean. See for yourself. No wrinkles. No age spots. Soft as a baby's."

Ketti looked at the hands crossed over the fairy godmother's chest. They were just as the rat had said, with long, slender fingers and nails like shiny, smooth seashells.

"I have always felt the beauty of their hands came from using wands," the rat went on. "All that magic channeling out would have to have its effect, I suppose."

Moving closer, Ketti strained to get a better view. Beneath the fairy godmother's hand was a wand, no more than eight inches long, and so polished that the grain seemed to jump out at Ketti.

"Go ahead," the rat said. "Take it. The godmother won't need it any longer, and we might. Too bad I don't know how to use it."

Ketti's fingers tingled as they met the wand. She gave a tug, but nothing happened. Then she tugged a little harder until, slowly, the wand glided out from under the fairy godmother's hands.

On impulse, Ketti squeezed her eyes shut, hit her head sharply with the wand three times and shouted, "Make me better than my sisters!"

Was there a glimmer of magic, or were the stars she saw on the inside of her lids from the force of the blows?

"Hush!" the rat scolded. "We don't want her to hear us."

"I thought she was"—the word came from Ketti's lips in a whisper—"dead."

"Oh, yes," the rat said. "The godmother is dead, but the other one is not."

"The other what? Is there another fairy godmother?"

The rat nodded, adding, "In fact, I have a cold suspicion that the rook—the black bird that flew out from the tree—was one of her spies. If we are to avoid Haduwig, we had best be off."

The strange name went through Ketti like a shudder. She followed the rat past a veil of leaves and into the sharp brilliance of a late-day autumn sun. "Is Haduwig our enemy?"

"I'm afraid she is," the rat answered. He began scurrying over a level expanse of green, heading for a dark forest and distant hills. Ketti saw no people, no houses, no wires or streetlights. There were no streets, either, not even a narrow path beaten bare by a cow. She tucked the lower half of the magic wand into a back pocket and hurried to catch up with the rat.

"What does this Haduwig have to do with the last spell you mentioned?"

"Nearly a hundred and fifteen years ago, a king invited twelve good fairies, godmothers, to bestow gifts on his princess daughter," the rat said, keeping up a steady trot. "Just before the last one could speak, a bad fairy, the witch named Haduwig, appeared. She was angry at not being invited."

Ketti picked up the story. " 'The princess,' she cried, 'shall, in her fifteenth year, prick her finger on a spindle and fall down dead!' "

The rat stopped in his tracks, his mouth agape. "How did you know?"

"It's Briar Rose's story. You know, Sleeping Beauty."

Ketti smiled, pleased with herself. "I mean, who else could it be?"

The rat shook his head in wonder. "The last fairy, the same godmother who lies beneath the tree back there, could not undo the spell. She could only hope to soften it."

Again Ketti leaped in. " 'The princess shall not die. She shall sleep in safety for a hundred years, until she can be woken by a prince's kiss of true love.' "

"Yes!" The rat stared up at Ketti, earnestness rounding his black eyes. "The hundred years are done at the rising of the next full moon, a fortnight from now. Haduwig has never gotten over having her spell diluted. She will do anything to see Briar Rose dead."

"And we will do anything to keep her from succeeding," Ketti vowed, starting to walk forward again. "So how do we start?"

"I rather hoped you would have the answer to that. I mean, the tree did send me to you."

Ketti thought as the rat kept pace alongside her. After a minute she asked, "Will Briar Rose be safe until the hundred years are up?"

"She will," the rat said.

"So then all we have to do is make sure a prince is around to kiss her at the very moment the spell ends. Once the spell is broken, you'll be a man—"

"And you'll get your wish—"

"And we'll all live happily ever after!" Ketti concluded.

# ✳ CHAPTER 4 ✳

## *Pancakes and Plans*

 A shady grove of pines stood at the end of the meadow. Bare of everything but pine needles, the ground gave off a sharp scent as Ketti stepped in alongside the rat. At first there were only pine trunks to see, and long, dripping lines of sap. But after some time, stumps dotted the ground, and they came to a place where split logs had been stacked between two close-growing trees.

Smelling wood smoke, Ketti stared with wide eyes until a splotch of yellow appeared through a break in the pines. As she and the rat neared it, it formed itself into a thatched roof covering a low, long building that had been whitewashed and framed with dark beams.

"Shoo!" a woman shouted as they emerged from the trees. Everything about her was rounded, from her cheeks and nose to her stomach and fingers. "You get out of my yard!"

The object of her fury was a goose. Not an ordinary goose, Ketti saw. It was colored gold, the shiny, buttery gold of a wedding ring, and it was headed for the deep-set doorway of the cottage. The woman waved her apron at it. When that didn't deter the bird, she picked up a broom. She used it, Ketti thought, the way a lion tamer wielded a chair.

"You get back, you hear? And do not be touching my broom!"

Ketti didn't understand what all the fuss was about. The goose was perfectly beautiful and seemed as tame as could be. It didn't hiss or spread its wings, as some geese would have. It simply toddled forward, looking silly and awkward.

"Maybe it's hungry," she suggested to the woman. But the woman was unmoved.

"Let it find its dinner someplace else."

Stepping toward the bird, Ketti decided to find out whether the feathers were soft like down or hard like metal. But the rat moved to cut her off, warning, "I wouldn't."

Before Ketti could ask why, a red-faced, stoop-shouldered man appeared. He reached into his vest pocket and pulled out a handful of stones.

"Oh, don't," Ketti protested.

He aimed at the ground a foot or so in front of the bird, shouting, "Be gone with you!" With each stone thrown, the goose backed farther away, moving closer to the edge of the pines. Then one pebble hit another and bounced wildly, striking the goose lightly on the breast. To Ketti's amazement, the stone stuck to the goose. Only then did she realize that the entire underside of the goose was covered with little bits of things, dirt and leaves and blades of grass, and even a small shoe.

"The golden goose," she said, understanding. "Everything sticks to it."

"Even you," the rat told her. "And then, in order to be free, you would have to search out a princess."

Ketti struggled to remember the fairy tale, of how a youngest son had found the goose at the root of a tree, of how a girl had been tempted to pet it and had gotten stuck, and how all who had tried to pull her free had become stuck, too.

"The boy walked past a princess with the goose and a whole string of people who couldn't get loose," Ketti said out loud. "When the princess saw them and laughed, the boy got to marry her and inherited the kingdom, didn't he?"

"Yes," the rat said. "But the important thing is that at the laugh, all came unstuck. Believe me, a laugh has saved many a life from misery. The problem now is finding a princess who has not already seen the goose and its foolishness. I'm afraid it is a very old joke."

With the goose gone, the man dropped the stones he had not thrown back into his vest pocket, saying, "Maybe the creature will go for good this time."

The woman lowered her broom. She motioned toward Ketti and the rat. "Hansel, dear, we have visitors."

Hansel? Why, he was white-haired and grizzled! Ketti turned to the round woman. "You're not—"

But she was. "I'm Gretel. Pleased to meet you."

"You're old!" Ketti said, surprise overriding her manners.

Gretel laughed. "Not as old as I'll be tomorrow."

Blushing, Ketti tried to explain. "I mean you're all grown up. How many years ago did you kill the witch?"

"Who keeps count?" Hansel asked.

"It was once upon a time," Gretel added. "But tell us who you are."

The rat made the introductions. Hansel and Gretel seemed more surprised to hear that Ketti was a girl than they were to hear the rat speak.

"Who has cut off your braids?" Gretel asked her. Hansel added, "Where is your dress?"

"Ketti comes from a faraway land where customs are different," the rat told them.

"Ah," the brother and sister said in unison. Then Gretel coaxed, "Come along inside. We were about to have a bite to eat."

"We can't," the rat said. "We're on our way to the sleeping castle. We have to see a fairy godmother's last spell through and make sure a certain witch doesn't interfere."

"But that's a long way off," Hansel told him. "And light's gone for the day. Best to stay with us tonight."

Glancing around, both Ketti and the rat saw that Hansel was right. The sun had slipped behind the hills. Although the sky was still lit, the trees that stood before it looked as flat and black as cutout silhouettes. After consulting each other with a look, they accepted Hansel and Gretel's invitation and stepped through the door into the cottage.

Inside, the air was smoky and dank. Everything was dim. At first all Ketti could make out was an open fireplace that took up much of one wall.

Hansel tapped Ketti's shoulder and pointed to a space above the door lintel. As Ketti's eyes adjusted to the dim light, she saw that a bone had been nailed there, an ancient-looking bone, whitened and knobby.

"You'll be safe from witches here," Hansel said. "That knucklebone keeps them away. It's a magic charm. Every day when the witch who penned me came to see how fat I was getting, I poked that charm at her." Hansel gestured with one hand. "Poke, poke. After a while, she went and leaped into an oven. Powerful charm, that."

When Ketti opened her mouth to protest it had been his sister who had pushed the witch into the oven, Gretel slid a stack of plates into her hands. "Will you set the table, Ketti Watson? Spoons and knives are over there."

"I'll fetch wood for later," Hansel said, grabbing a cap from a peg near the door. "Come along and keep me company, rat."

With the bang of the door, Ketti set out plates and spoons and knives. The utensils were made of something like pewter. The plates were wood, carved and rubbed smooth, dark with years of use.

"I see you have a wand," Gretel said. She was leveling the embers under an iron cooking stand.

Ketti pulled the tapered stick from her pocket. "The problem is, we don't know how to use it." After watching Gretel tip a clay pitcher over a frying pan, she asked, "Why don't you tell?"

Gretel laughed. "Me? I don't know how to use a wand."

"No," Ketti said, putting the wand away again. "I mean Hansel. Why don't you tell him it was you who pushed the witch into the oven?"

Gretel smiled. Her face reflected the red of the coals. She looked younger than before, and prettier. "I like him to be happy."

"Even if it means he gets credit for something you did?"

"Oh, you know how it is between a brother and sister."

"I only have sisters."

"It's the same, I'm sure. Sometimes you want to do something or say something just to please them. Then you're happy, too."

Thinking resentfully of Ellen getting new puppets and Miranda traveling to Florida again, Ketti couldn't agree.

"Back then," Gretel went on, "Hansel was the

special one—older he was, and more clever. I was a bit of a baby, I'm afraid, whimpering whenever he teased me or ran off with my doll. Cry is all I did when we discovered our parents were plotting to lose us in the forest. It was Hansel who thought of the stones and got us home again."

"And it was Hansel who thought of the bread crumbs and got you lost," Ketti reminded her.

"But he meant to do well. And he was already coming undone." Gretel twisted as if to be sure Hansel was not yet returning. The thick, wavy glass of the windows was black with night. "After our stay with the witch, he was never the same. He carries pebbles in his pockets to drop, lest he lose his way, and he won't permit an oven on the premises, not even the tiniest oven, one whose door wouldn't admit the head of a baby. How I do long for a good, crusty loaf of bread. But hush. He's back. Do not repeat a word of this. I couldn't bear for him to be unhappy."

It was a simple dinner of pancakes and sugar, milk, apples, and nuts. As they ate, a coolness grew in the room. When Hansel got up to move the cooking stand and set a fire blazing, Ketti was glad.

"Nice to have company," Gretel murmured.

Hansel pulled a stool up to tend the fire. "Sometimes Gretel will go for months without seeing a new face. Now me"—he assumed an air of worldliness—"I go to the city once a month to sell my wood. But for a change of pace, poor Gretel has to hope for peddlers."

"Or fortune seekers," Gretel said, breaking in, "like you two. I suppose you've heard about the terrible plague of thorns."

"Thorns?" the rat repeated.

"Around the sleeping castle," Gretel said, "where you said you're bound. Evil work, that. No one will be able to get in there now. Hansel heard the thorns hold fast to any who venture into them, as though they had hands. And it's said they have surrounded the castle so that nothing can be seen of it, not even the flagpoles on the roof."

Ketti had forgotten about the thorns in the story. Had they only appeared with the fairy godmother's death? Were they the start of Haduwig's magic against them? After mulling those thoughts over, Ketti considered an even larger problem.

"Just where are we going to find a prince to take to Briar Rose?" she asked the rat.

As the rat and Ketti fell into troubled silence, Hansel picked up a crude poker to prod the failing fire. As if scratching the belly of a big, lazy dog, he scraped the underside of the log, coaxing it slowly back into flame.

"I know where all the princes are," he said slowly. "They've gathered in a city not far out of your way in order to answer a proclamation. You would have dozens to choose from. You see, a king has announced that whoever can answer his question may choose a wife from among his daughters and reign after his death."

Ketti asked, "What's the question?"

Hansel smiled shyly. "To tell the truth, I didn't listen closely. It's a matter for princes."

Gretel encouraged him, saying, "You must remember something, Hansel. Tell the girl whatever you know."

"I know this much: The king is Birandell and the princes have gone to his city to stay at the Thirsty Mug. The mystery itself has something to do with worn-out clothes. Many princes have tried to solve it. So far, all have failed and have paid with their lives." Hansel leaned toward Ketti and drew a finger across his neck. "Heads chopped off!"

Seeing Ketti pale, Gretel laid an arm around her shoulders. "Poor thing. Hansel has upset you."

"It . . . it's all right," Ketti said. "He's been a big help. At least we know now where to find a prince. Tomorrow we'll go to that city."

"Dressed like that?" Gretel exclaimed.

Ketti imagined Gretel was concerned about her lack of a dress. But when Gretel opened a chest, she brought out a bundle of dark, rough cloth. "Take this with you."

"What is it?" Ketti asked.

With a snap, Gretel unfurled a hooded cape. For a moment the garment rippled gracefully. Then its hem thudded to the floor, leaving dust motes dancing in the firelight. "This cloak was left behind by a fortune seeker," Gretel said. "You'll be a day and a half on the road to King Birandell's city, so you'll be glad of its warmth when you're out at night."

"And speaking of night," the rat said, "it's time Ketti was in bed."

It was a tiny room Gretel led her into, furnished with a bed and a rickety table holding a pitcher and bowl. There was just one small window, high up on the wall. Through it, Ketti saw the moon, thin as a sliver, and she remembered the rat's words: "The hundred years are done at the rising of the next full moon—"

Gretel broke into Ketti's thoughts, pulling a sock from beneath her apron. Its contents jingled as she emptied it into Ketti's hands.

"Hansel usually makes trades for the wood he chops—a string of sausages, a bag of flour—but sometimes he gets paid with coins. I ask you, where am I to spend them? You take these and use them well."

"Thank you," Ketti said solemnly.

"Now here's water for washing up," Gretel added, pointing to the pitcher, "and I'll be back with a second blanket. Night can be cold this time of year."

But if Gretel returned, Ketti didn't know it. After she'd punched the straw of her mattress into shape and wrapped herself in a feather comforter, she fell fast asleep and didn't wake until dawn.

# ✳ CHAPTER 5 ✳
## *A Pact and Some Panic*

The next morning, Ketti and the rat started off on the first leg of their journey, stocked with provisions of food. Since the day was mild, Ketti didn't wear the cloak Gretel had given her. She rolled it into a tight, sausage-shaped bundle and draped it around her neck. With her thoughts on princes and King Birandell's city, she followed the rat all day, out of the pine grove, across a shallow river, over a wooded hill, and down the length of a boggy valley.

Finally they sat together in a boulder-strewn clearing to eat. After setting down the cloak and checking her pockets to be sure the wand and the coins were safe, Ketti offered the rat his portion of dinner: a piece of cheese and some cold pancakes.

"I've been wondering about something," she said.

"If the godmother was already dead when you came through the wormhole and you don't know how to use the wand, how did you keep me out of trouble at home?"

"Oh," the rat said, coughing. "That worked, did it?"

"What do you mean?"

"If everything worked out, there is no need . . ." The rat's brow grew furrowed. "Have I mentioned that time is against us? We have only until the full moon—"

"You're trying to change the subject," Ketti said. "It won't work, so explain yourself."

When the rat spoke, his voice was almost inaudible. "I had no power to help you. If you stayed out of trouble that day, it was due to luck or to something you did."

Ketti swallowed the food in her mouth with difficulty. "You lied? You lied to me?"

"I am not proud," the rat confessed. "I could think of no other way to get what I needed."

"What you needed? But I trusted you. You told me if I came back again you would keep me out of trouble. It was a bargain. We made a deal and . . . and you cheated!"

The rat grew defensive. "And I suppose you have never lied or cheated?"

The words lie and cheat jabbed at Ketti uncomfortably. She had met the rat when she'd been cheating at hide-and-seek. A lie had kept her out of trouble at home. But she'd never imagined how terrible it was to be on the other side. To push away her guilty feelings, she lashed out at the rat again.

"Next thing, you'll be telling me you can't get me my happily-ever-after."

When the rat looked away, Ketti's heart began to pound. "Well, can you?"

After pawing some crumbs of cheese on the ground, he murmured, "It is not exactly assured."

Ketti began to gather up the cloak and the food. She would leave the rat, she decided. Her legs were longer and she could travel faster. She could beat him to King Birandell's city and the sleeping castle, and the fairy godmother's promise would go to her.

"Don't follow me," she warned. "And don't try to keep up!"

The rat ran frantic circles around her. "Do you hear it? Ketti, stop and listen! Do you hear it?"

"I won't stay with you another moment," Ketti ranted. She could hear it now. Something was moving through the underbrush. "I'm getting my happily-ever-after no matter what." Something was rustling leaves, breaking branches, trampling twigs, and heading for them.

"*Wonk, wonk, a-wonk!*" With wings spread, the golden goose burst into the clearing.

"Do not be caught!" the rat shouted.

Ketti clutched the cloak to her chest and ran.

"*Wonk, wonk!*" the goose cried as it flapped after her.

It was fast. Ketti felt the breath of its wings on her heels. What would it be like to be stuck to a goose?

And what if the goose were a biter? Rushing into the trees, Ketti could almost feel the pinch of the goose's big golden beak.

"*Wonk, wonk, a-wonk!*"

"I can't—" Ketti meant to say that she couldn't go on any longer, but she was too out of breath to get the words out. There was pain in her side like a knife pushing in and out of her ribs.

"Go on!" the rat insisted.

Soon they were deep in the wood, running through the shadows of the surrounding hills. After splashing through a bubbling stream, Ketti turned, completely exhausted, to watch the goose fall upon her. It was unavoidable. It was inevitable. It was—

"Gone," Ketti gasped. "It's gone."

Puffing, she dropped to the ground. The rat collapsed beside her. It was several minutes before he could talk.

"I wish you had given me a chance to speak before," he managed finally. "I have always meant to get you your happily-ever-after. That is why I had you take the godmother's wand. True, I do not know how to use it, but surely Cinderella will. She was certainly present when it was used. We will stop at her palace after we find a prince. It is on our way to Briar Rose, in any event. Are we friends again?"

Ketti wasn't sure she could find King Birandell's city or the sleeping castle on her own and nodded grudgingly. "Friends," she agreed. "But I'd better get my happily-ever-after, and no more lies!"

The rat held up one paw to swear his sincerity. "It

shall be a pact between us: No more lies."

"And no more cheating!"

"No more—" The rat broke off to think. "We have to cheat one more time, Ketti, to cheat Haduwig out of her curse. But that's it. Then there will be no more cheating."

With the sun gone, the sky melted from azure to indigo and they settled in for the night. Worried about the return of the golden goose, the rat retreated to the branch of a tree. Ketti, more fearful of falling, remained on the ground. She was surprised at how comfortable she was, once she had cocooned the cloak and its hood around herself. In almost no time, she fell into a deep, dreamless slumber.

It was in the coldest hour of the night that Ketti woke with a jolt, her heart pounding inexplicably with fear. The wood around her was silver with the light of stars shining in a black, faraway sky. Trees swayed gently. The stream gurgled. Leaves, dry and brown, rattled as they clung stubbornly to branches. Everything was as it should have been. And yet . . .

Something was out there.

With that thought, a wave of terror swept over Ketti. Get up. Run, a voice inside her urged.

Ketti shook her head to be rid of such foolishness. Sighing, she shifted, stiff from lying too long in one position. She closed her eyes. And immediately the feeling was with her again.

Something was after her.

Ketti's eyes flicked open. Wildly, she searched the

wood, but she could find nothing out of the ordinary.

Then it came: *Sniff.*

At the sound, Ketti went cold. The hair rose on the back of her neck. Run, the voice urged again, but Ketti held still.

*Sniff.*

Whatever it was, it was moving closer. The rat? The goose? Ketti pulled the cloak closer around herself as a black figure appeared just yards from where she lay. From the shape, Ketti guessed it to be a woman—an old woman, huddled with age, and a poor woman, swathed in dark rags. Certainly no one to be afraid of, Ketti told herself. But as the woman's head turned slowly from side to side, Ketti was filled with a pure, unreasoning terror.

Sniff. Sniff.

The woman was hidden by a cowl, but her face lifted as she smelled the air. It was as if she were searching, searching for a particular, elusive scent.

The woman shuffled forward, one step, two. Then, to Ketti's horror, she began shrinking. No, Ketti realized in a panic. Not shrinking. Lowering herself to the ground, leaning on something like a walking stick to get down on her hands and knees. It seemed she'd caught a whiff of whatever it was she was looking for. She began crawling purposefully toward Ketti.

Ketti was shaking inside the cloak. She was certain, as certain as she'd ever been of anything in her life, that the woman was evil, and yet she found she couldn't move a muscle to get away.

The head lifted again, this time revealing two red eyes blazing from the darkness of the cowl. All at once they appeared to lock on Ketti, who stifled a gasp with her hand. But then there came another sniff. Seeming unsure, the woman inched forward, a little to the right of where Ketti lay. When she stopped, a pair of white hands emerged from the loose sleeves of her garment. They were beautiful hands, well shaped and smooth, with long, sharp fingernails. But as Ketti watched, they changed. The thumbs drew toward the little fingers until they resembled two hooked claws, two savage rakes that began striking the ground. Dirt and moss and leaves tumbled from the woman's fingers as she brought each handful up to her face. And each handful she grabbed brought her closer to Ketti.

She'll tear into me the same way and there's nothing I can do, Ketti thought.

But inches away from discovering Ketti, the woman froze. A sound like a battle cry was echoing through the wood.

"*Wonk, wonk, a-wonk!*"

Trumpeting loudly, the golden goose appeared, waving wings burnished with starlight. Ketti almost cheered when the old woman fell back helpless before it. But all too soon the woman was pushing to her feet, raising her thin arms above her head, mixing the air with a broom as if calling up all the forces of evil.

"*Yawahtiwuoy!*" she commanded.

Ketti's hands flew to her ears. She was certain the

bird would shrivel before the awful jangle of sounds. But "*Wonk!*" the goose blared, pressing forward. And to Ketti's astonishment, the woman began moving away. In moments, she had disappeared as silently as she'd come. One name repeated itself in Ketti's mind: Haduwig.

"Ketti Watson!" a familiar voice hissed. "Where are you?"

Still wrapped in the hooded cloak, Ketti sat up to greet the rat as he dropped from a tree near the stream.

"Oh, where are you?" he asked in a plaintive whine, running right past her. "Why did I leave you alone?"

"I'm here," she said. Curious, she watched as the rat turned and scanned the very spot where she sat.

"Ketti?"

"Right here. What's the matter with you?"

"There's nothing the matter with me. But you . . ." The rat swallowed. "You have been disembodied!"

"What?" For an instant, Ketti wondered if the witch had really gotten her, if the deadly claws had somehow destroyed her without pain. But then she threw back the cloak and laughed. "I'm here. I'm fine."

"Great galumphing giants!"

"What? What is it?" Ketti looked down, patting her own solidness.

"You . . . you weren't there a moment ago."

"Don't be silly. Of course I was."

The rat shook his head. "I couldn't see you."

Something clicked in Ketti's mind. The witch hadn't seen her, either. Those awful red eyes might have been weak, but they weren't blind. On impulse, she pulled the hooded cloak around herself again.

"You are a ghost!" the rat exclaimed.

"*OooOOOooo!*" Ketti howled delightedly, wrapping and unwrapping herself again and again. The rat backed away, frightened, until Ketti sat uncovered for him to see her again.

"It's the cloak," she said. "It makes me invisible! When I'm inside, even the cloak itself disappears, and that's why Haduwig didn't find me. Oh, she would have in another second, if it hadn't been for the goose—"

As if on cue, the golden goose waddled into the space beside the rat. The rat jumped and then raced up the nearest tree.

"Move away!" he warned. "Hurry!"

The goose, shoe still clinging to its bottom, settled to the ground in front of Ketti.

"I think it's all right," she said.

The bird wiggled harmlessly from side to side to make a nest in some moss.

"See? It won't do anything to me. It saved me." She smiled at the goose and nodded. "Thank you."

When the goose responded with a series of soft honks, Ketti told the rat, "I think it means to stay and protect me."

Cautiously, the rat returned to the ground. "It is perhaps the only creature that Haduwig fears," he admitted. "Before this goose, she is no different than the rest of us. And think: What princess is brave enough to laugh at the sight of Haduwig, stuck to a goose or not?

For the rest of her days, Haduwig would be condemned to go about with that animal glued to her side."

Ketti rolled up the cloak once more, then got up to splash some water from the stream onto her face. After such a visit, there would be no more sleep.

The rat predicted, "If we leave now, we shall collect our prince before lunch." Leading the way along the stream bank, he sang out, "To King Birandell's city and happily-ever-after!"

"To happily-ever-after," Ketti echoed, and the golden goose fell into step behind her.

As they walked, the stars faded. A hint of pink rose behind the trees in the east and the sun came soon after, seemingly born, red and sleepy, from a distant hill. Once free of the horizon, the sun quickly turned yellow—lighting the sky, warming the air—and the wood itself came alive with bird sounds.

"Swans," Ketti announced as they reached the place where the stream emptied into a lake.

Through a mist that hovered over the calm water like so many ghosts, a family of swans dipped their bills, paddled, and, bottom side up, fished for breakfast. To Ketti's dismay, the golden goose decided to join them. As it slipped into the water, a honey-colored wake rippled out behind it.

"Oh, don't go!" Ketti pleaded. "I need you!"

Who else would protect her from Haduwig? Who else could?

# CHAPTER 6

# *Roswald and Pollock*

Midmorning, Ketti stood with the rat on a hillside and looked down on King Birandell's huge, wall-encircled city. Somewhere in that mass of slanting roofs and turrets was a prince, she thought. Briar Rose's prince.

"Just where do you suppose the Thirsty Mug is?" she asked, recalling the place where Hansel had said the princes were gathered.

The rat reminded Ketti it would be up to her to find it. For safety's sake, he would ride, invisible, on her back. "I will not be welcomed in the city," he had explained. "Visible, I shall only attract catcalls and cudgels."

So at the side of a well-traveled track, the first sign of a road Ketti had seen, she rerolled the cloak with the rat inside. As soon as it had closed around him, the cloak disappeared along with the rat. Ketti lifted the invisible garment to her back and noted that, rolled, it had no effect on her.

"Are you okay in there?" she asked.

The rat's answer was a muffled complaint of cramped quarters and stuffiness. "But I shall endure," he finished. "Let us be off for the city."

The route Ketti followed was no more than a path formed by the pounding of many feet. Unpaved, muddy, and edged with wheel ruts, it was narrow at first. But it grew steadily broader as Ketti went, becoming widest just outside the city wall. There it ended in a gateway that was guarded by soldiers in dirty red uniforms. Their job, it appeared, was to stop each person and decide whether or not entry to the city would be granted.

"What brings you to King Birandell's city?" one asked when Ketti stepped forward to take her turn. Awaiting an answer, he blocked her way with the blade of his unsheathed sword.

"I . . . I'm going to the Thirsty Mug," Ketti stammered.

"On what business?"

"To see the princes."

"You're too late," a second soldier said from the other side of the gateway. He let one peasant with a sack of carrots pass by and stopped another who pulled a rickety two-wheeled cart. "Today's execution is over," he told Ketti. "It's always held at dawn. Come again in three days. There's sure to be another."

"I want to see the live princes," Ketti explained.

Grudgingly the first soldier moved his sword, but

as he did so, the end of it found the invisible cloak where it sat atop Ketti's right shoulder. Before she could prevent it, the cloak had fallen to the ground somewhere behind her. Instead of moving on so that the next person could be questioned, Ketti spun around and dropped to her knees.

"What are you doing?" the soldier demanded.

Ketti's hands patted the ground frantically, searching without finding the cloak. "I've lost something!"

"Move on or you'll find my blade," he warned her.

The second soldier stamped toward Ketti, threatening, "If she dares to pass these gates, I'll throw her out on her ear!"

"You'll do no such thing," said a new voice.

Ketti looked up gratefully into the face of a handsome, bearded stranger, a third soldier she had not seen before. Apparently a visitor to the city, he wore the green uniform of another army. Smiling, he asked, "Can I help you, little one?"

At that very moment, Ketti's fingers brushed something coarse. In seconds, she had gathered up the invisible rolled cloak, bunched it to her chest, and run on into the city.

King Birandell's city had looked large from a distance. Even so, Ketti wasn't prepared for the number of streets. Dark, narrow, and twisting, they were as crowded with houses as they were with people. Buildings hemmed both sides of the roadways, almost meeting above Ketti's head. Second stories overlapped first, third stories stuck out beyond second, and so on, making the structures look like overturned wedding cakes. Although there was no motor traffic, the city was every bit as noisy and smelly as any of the modern ones Ketti had visited. In fact, it was worse. Piles of rotting garbage marked the corners and alleyways. And mixing with the odor of decay was that of unwashed people, most of whom seemed to be shouting.

"Sweets, here! Sweets!"

"Good jelly to sell!"

"Alms for the poor! Alms, please!"

"Do you see the Thirsty Mug?" the rat whispered from his hiding place.

Ketti, like a street mime, was already attracting stares as she straightened the rolled-up, invisible cloak and settled it once more around her shoulders. After clearing her throat meaningfully, she murmured, "Give me a few minutes to look around."

But as it turned out, the rat had much longer to wait. It wasn't until noontime that Ketti announced success. She found the inn tucked into a lane guttered on one side by a trickle of brackish water. Stepping carefully, she went into a room bustling with people and talk and laughter.

"Go on!" bawled a rumpled, dough-faced man. "Go on with you! That's not your husband! I won't believe it."

He was talking to a crone of a woman, toothless and humpbacked. A rope ran from her hand to the neck of a pig, brown with caked mud.

"It is," she swore. "It is my husband."

The pig flicked its head. Ketti wasn't sure if it was agreeing with the woman or simply chasing a fly from its ear.

"Was one of those little woodmen what changed him," the woman said, "for not sharing his dinner, the little he had. It's a crime, I say. Somebody ought to do something. How am I supposed to live? 'Twas my man what supported us by chopping wood. I ask you, how's he to hold the ax now?"

"It isn't my problem," the dough-faced man said without feeling. "Now begone! I welcome no beggars here."

Ketti decided he was the innkeeper. She watched him fill a tankard from a big wooden keg and hand it to a waiting peasant. His eyes narrowed greedily as he snatched up the money he received in payment.

"What do you want?" he roared when he spied Ketti. "If you've come begging, your pleas will fall on deaf ears."

"No," Ketti said, finding her voice with difficulty. "I've come to see the princes."

"I don't put up with beggars or sightseers."

Shaking, Ketti dug a coin out of her pocket and held it up to the innkeeper's face. "I'll pay!"

Although she had no idea of its worth, the innkeeper did. His eyes lit up at the sight and, in a twinkling, the coin had moved from Ketti's hand to the inside of his purse.

"This way," he said, leading Ketti through a short

passageway. "You may not only see the princes, you may sup with them. And if you're interested, another coin will get you a room. I'm sure I'll have one free. Business is bound to slack off for a couple of days. We won't be packed again until the next head-chopping—oh, I beg your royal pardons. That was unkind of me."

They had reached a cozy dining room, where a cheery fire blazed and blue curtains hung at the leaded windows. The table, covered by white linen, was dotted here and there with silver-rimmed dishes. Around it were high-backed, carved chairs. Two of them were occupied by men.

"Quite all right," the gentlemen said in response to the innkeeper's apology.

The woman waiting table ladled soup into bowls. Ketti set the cloak down gently on an empty chair and took a seat beside it. "Where are the rest of you?" she asked.

"The rest of us?" said the fairer of the two men.

"You're the princes, aren't you?" Smelling the food, Ketti realized she was starving and dipped a spoon into the steaming bowl that had been placed before her. The soup was cabbage, a kind she'd have refused at home. On an empty stomach, it tasted heavenly.

"I need a prince," she said between sips, "and I have a deal to offer. I figure it would be easiest if I could talk to all of you together."

"Prince Roswald, Prince Pollock, this is . . ." The innkeeper turned to Ketti questioningly.

"Ketti Watson," she said, putting down the spoon to hold out her hand.

"How d'you do?" the princes said in unison.

They weren't Ketti's ideas of princes. True, their clothes were gorgeous, woven with threads of gold and studded with jewels. But they themselves were quite ordinary. The one called Roswald was on the short side and heavy, with a mottled, ruddy complexion. Pollock was taller and fair but skinny, with a sunken chest and thick lips.

"I'm afraid we are all of us," Prince Roswald said in answer to Ketti's question. "All of us who are left."

While the woman removed the soup bowl and replaced it with a platter of ham and turnips, Ketti said carefully, "I was told there'd be dozens of you."

"Oh, there were," Prince Pollock said, patting his mouth delicately with a napkin. "But this mystery of the princesses is troublesome."

"Terribly troublesome," Prince Roswald agreed.

"So the rest of you are . . ." Ketti started to put a finger up to her throat but thought better of it.

"Passed on to a finer world," Prince Roswald said.

"You don't need to risk your lives," Ketti said slowly. "I know of another way to win a princess and a kingdom."

The princes chuckled politely.

"I'm serious," she said. "I know of a princess who's under a spell. If you wake her, you'll get to marry her."

"Wake her, wake her." Prince Pollock tapped a finger

against his fleshy lower lip. "That seems to ring a bell."

Prince Roswald clapped his hands. "Briar Rose, that's who she means!"

"That's who I mean," Ketti confirmed. Again the princes laughed. Ketti fidgeted in her chair.

"Listen," she said. "All you have to do is—"

Prince Roswald stopped her. "Sorry. Not I."

"What do you mean?"

"Not I," he repeated.

"Nor I," said Pollock.

"But why?" Ketti wanted to know.

Prince Roswald pushed his chair back from the table and folded his hands over his large waist. "Shall I tell her or shall you, Pollock?"

"You begin and I shall speak whenever I think of something to add."

"Very good," Roswald said. He held up one plump finger. "First of all, Ketti Watson, there's never been a proclamation. Nobody has ever asked a prince to rescue Briar Rose."

"Her family is asleep, too," Pollock reminded, arranging his napkin beside his plate.

"Second," Roswald went on, holding up two fingers, "even if her family would appreciate a prince's efforts at waking her up, there's no kingdom left for a reward."

"Oh, I'm sure you're wrong about that," Ketti started to say, but Roswald smiled knowingly.

"A hundred years is a long time. Several lifetimes, in fact. Let me fill you in on a little history, my girl.

After Briar Rose and the castle folk fell asleep, people began moving in on their kingdom, taking the land right from under their snoring noses, you might say. It wasn't thievery, exactly. Each one simply thought, I'll be dead before they wake. They won't mind or even know if I borrow a bit of land. Of course, their children came along and their grandchildren and their great-grandchildren. And pretty soon the whole countryside was built up with cottages and farms and the like. The land was free, none of it taxed. Frankly, all of it has been used for so long that if some king suddenly wakes up and demands his rights, there'll be a fearsome fight!"

"I'd rather solve a princess puzzle," said Prince Pollock, yawning.

"But—"

Prince Roswald held up three fingers. "Thirdly, Ketti Watson, gossip has it that, while Briar Rose has been sleeping, she has gone right on aging."

"No, she hasn't!"

"Have you seen her?"

Ketti had to shake her head.

"Lads have sneaked into the castle from time to time," Prince Roswald explained. "They've brought out frightful tales of white hair filling rooms, of fingernails longer than quill pens, of a face all caved in, of teeth rotted out and a body like a skeleton."

"All lies!" Ketti declared angrily.

"By my calculations," Roswald said, "Briar Rose ought to be about a hundred and fifteen now."

Prince Pollock rubbed his eyes sleepily. "I could never marry a woman older than myself."

"So you see, Ketti Watson," Roswald concluded, getting to his feet, "we're telling you the truth when we say we're simply not the right princes for this task. But thank you for your pleasant dinner company."

As the two men headed for the door, Ketti pressed her face into her hands. Without a prince, any hope of happily-ever-after was lost.

The moon that night was thicker than it had been the night Ketti arrived. It was a white crescent tipped over the darkened and emptied streets below her room in the Thirsty Mug.

"I bet that's just what Haduwig's mouth looks like tonight," Ketti told the rat. "A big old satisfied grin. We came all this way, and for what? There are only two princes left. One of them is off tonight to try and solve the mystery at the castle, and neither of them is willing to wake up Briar Rose."

Relieved to be free of the cloak, the rat stretched out on a narrow mattress, the room's only furnishing.

"Which prince has gone to the castle?" he asked.

Ketti didn't know. "Does it matter? Neither of them are exactly Prince Charming."

"Perhaps Briar Rose doesn't need a prince," the rat suggested.

Ketti turned away from the window, shaking her head. "Her true love is a prince. I know because it's in the fairy tale. Believe me, I know all the fairy tales. I act them out with puppets for my sister Ellen. That's how I know about you and Cinderella and Briar Rose and Hansel and Gretel and the golden goose. Maybe that's why the fairy godmother sent you to me."

The rat was thoughtful. "Could the princess puzzle be in a fairy tale as well?"

Ketti considered. "Not everything around here is. The lady and the pig I saw before, they're like a fairy tale gone wrong. And King Birandell doesn't sound familiar at all."

"Perhaps you do not have enough details," the rat said. "If we could find out more and you could solve the mystery—"

Ketti caught on. "If we could solve the mystery for the prince in the castle, there'd still be one prince here in the Thirsty Mug. And with nothing left for him to gain, he just might come with us to Briar Rose!"

# ✳ CHAPTER 7 ✳

## *All in a Row*

 As one day followed another, Ketti and the rat sought information. The best they could learn was that each prince had three nights to solve a mystery that had something to do with princesses and worn-out clothing.

Ketti was at a loss.

"It's not much," the rat conceded.

As to which prince was in the castle, no one seemed to know. Once Ketti tried to get in to see him, but she couldn't get close to the royal residence. A thick wall surrounded the complex and behind it stood a huge fortified tower, which the rat called a donjon. The sole glimpse Ketti got into the enclave was through an iron-grilled portcullis. Sadly, she had to admit to both the rat and herself that their only hope was for the prince to solve the mystery on his own.

On the morning after the third night, the streets filled with people all moving in the same direction. With the rat once again wrapped inside the rolled-up cloak and the cloak invisible, draped around her neck, Ketti melted into the flow. Soon she found herself in a large square, not far from the castle walls, where two wooden platforms had been erected. One sat off to the side while the other occupied a more central position. Before long, a blare of horns heralded a procession arriving on horseback. Leading them all was Prince Roswald.

"I think we're in luck," Ketti whispered to the rat. "The prince is first in line, and he's all dressed up. Maybe he succeeded!"

Like actors in a play, the members of the procession found their places in the square. Ketti watched Roswald take center stage while the others were ushered into seats on the side platform. That was when Ketti began to worry.

"He doesn't look happy," she hissed to the rat. "Why doesn't he look happy?"

"HEAR YE, HEAR YE!" someone began. "HIS MOST ROYAL HIGHNESS KING BIRANDELL THE BOLD REGRETS—"

Ketti closed her eyes. She didn't want to know what was coming next. She'd seen the man with the ax.

There were no drum rolls, no final words or pleas for mercy. Ketti knew that the deed was done only when a gasp escaped the assembled crowd. Without meaning to, she opened her eyes. What she focused on was not the slain Roswald but a girl on the side platform, a girl not much older than herself in a flowing dress edged with fur. She wore a gold chaplet on her head, but Ketti's attention was caught by what the girl wore on her feet: They were the brightest, newest shoes Ketti had ever seen. Unless she counted the shoes on the somewhat taller girl beside the first. Her shoes were new, too. And so were the shoes of the next girl and the next and the next, all the way down the row to the last. A smile played around the edges of this last young woman's mouth. Shaking, Ketti lifted up a finger to count. Twelve. Twelve princesses in a row, twelve princesses in new shoes.

"I know the fairy tale!" Ketti cried out. "The mystery isn't about worn-out clothes, it's about worn-out shoes. It's 'The Twelve Dancing Princesses'!"

"Now you know?" the rat said. Even muffled by the invisible cloak, his voice sounded bitter. "It is a bit late to be of any assistance to us, although I suppose you could spare Prince Pollock's life, if you wished. Now when he goes to the castle, he will be able to solve the mystery. Unfortunately that leaves no prince for us."

"Oh, I'll spare Pollock's life," Ketti said confidently. "But he'll be coming with us. What we have to do is find a soldier."

Ketti scanned the retreating mob until her eyes stopped on a familiar-looking green uniform outside a baker's shop. "Excuse me, sir!" she called, running after him.

The kind soldier from the gate seemed amused when Ketti caught up with him. "Did you find whatever it was you were looking for?" he asked.

Ketti put up a hand to smooth her hair, realizing she hadn't combed it since she'd left home. "Um, yes," she said awkwardly. "It's a cloak and it's for you."

Seeing nothing, the soldier smiled tolerantly. "That's kind of you, little one. Here. Eat a piece of this muffin."

Ketti nibbled gratefully, thinking what a terrible shame it was that the soldier wasn't a prince. He seemed perfect for Briar Rose. After swallowing, she did her best to remember the story of the twelve dancing princesses and blurted out, "How would you like to find out where the king's daughters wear their shoes into tatters? How would you like to become king?"

The soldier laughed. Ketti thought it was the nicest laugh she had ever heard. "Yes, little one. That is a good idea. I shall do so as soon as I finish my breakfast."

"But the king wants to know where his daughters go at night," Ketti insisted, "and I know the answer."

"And how do you know?" the soldier asked, brushing the crumbs from his hands.

"I can't tell you that. You'll have to trust me. Do you trust me?"

Narrowing his eyes, the soldier nodded slowly. "It is foolishness I am sure, but I do trust you."

"Good," Ketti said. "This is what you have to do. Go to the king—"

"Will he allow a poor soldier to vie for one of his daughters?"

"He will," Ketti said. "I don't know why, but he will. Perhaps he will believe that all the princes are dead."

"And if this last prince I have heard of arrives—"

"You've just got to get to the castle before him. Anyhow, the king will take you to a room next to his daughters' bedroom so you can watch them. And this is important: Don't drink the wine they bring you."

The soldier nodded again, speaking softly. "Then the wine is drugged."

"You have to make believe you're asleep," Ketti went on, "and when the princesses start leaving, you have to wear this."

Ducking her head, she brought the rolled-up invisible cloak forward.

"Free me first," the rat whispered.

Hearing him, the soldier backed away, asking, "What manner of sorcery is this?"

"It's not sorcery," Ketti said. "It's my friend."

The cloak appeared as Ketti unwrapped the rat. The rat appeared, too. When he hurried across the un-paved ground and up a wall to the safety of a roof, the soldier's eyes went wide.

"Why should I think it strange to be king," he asked, "when there is a child such as you who travels with a ghostly rat?"

Ketti grinned. And saying, "Just do everything like I told you," she shoved the cloak into his arms.

✳　✳　✳

Three nights later, when the rat moaned, "Our time is half gone," Ketti almost added that their money was completely gone. Only moments before, she had given the innkeeper the last of Gretel's coins. One way or another, it was their final night in King Birandell's city. But Ketti didn't want to worry the rat. She leaned on the windowsill of their room and tried to reassure him.

"We have to wait for the soldier to succeed or we won't stand a chance of convincing Prince Pollock to come along with us."

"And if he still won't?"

Ketti didn't dare think of that possibility. She looked up at the half-moon, gleaming in a sky like black velvet, and whispered, "He has to."

# CHAPTER 8

# *One Step Closer*

The cry was heard all through the Thirsty Mug and out into the lane. Ketti and King Birandell's messenger were the only ones close enough to make out the choked words that followed.

"My brother's throne will rock with his laughter," Prince Pollock sobbed. "First the humiliation of a common soldier taking my place at the castle. And now to hear that he has succeeded—I shall never recover!"

Ketti paced the hallway until the messenger had gone. Then she knocked softly on the door to the prince's room.

"Go away!" he called out.

Ignoring his order, she pushed the door open. The room behind it was dark. Ketti's eyes skimmed over a pallet, several trunks, and a disheveled bed to find

Prince Pollock standing near a window that had been covered with a fur-lined mantle. The prince was muttering to himself.

"Bested by a soldier, a common soldier. A laughingstock is what I am."

"I take it the soldier has told the king where the princesses wear out their shoes," Ketti said, stepping into the room.

"They dance with twelve young men in an underground castle."

Ketti nodded. "I know."

"It was my turn," the prince whined, twisting to face her. With his shoulders hunched forward, his sunken chest seemed more pronounced than ever. "I should have been the one to find out. I should have been the one to become King Birandell's heir. It's not fair!"

"Without help you wouldn't have figured it out," Ketti said gently. "You would have had your head chopped off."

Prince Pollock stamped his foot petulantly. "You don't understand! All my life, my father's court has treated my brother better than me, just because he's older. I am every bit as good as he. Better! But will I inherit our father's kingdom? No. Simply because I was not born first."

"It isn't fair," Ketti agreed, thinking of Miranda.

"Here in this city," Prince Pollock went on, "I thought to find fortune and the respect of my brother. But I have failed."

"There's still another way," Ketti reminded. "There's still Briar Rose."

The prince made a noise of disgust.

"I'm telling you," Ketti said, "she's not old and her family will be thrilled when you've woken her up. Maybe her kingdom won't be as big as your brother's, but so what? It will be something. And you won't have gotten it because you had the luck to be born first. You'll have earned it. It might even be your happily-ever-after."

"Happily ever after," the prince repeated. He spoke the words like a man lost in a dream.

When a servant appeared, he set a tray on the bed and tucked a napkin under Prince Pollock's chin. "Your breakfast, sire."

The prince seemed to rouse himself. "Henry, I leave this place today."

"Very good," Henry answered. "I know your father will be pleased to have you back."

"No, Henry," the prince said. "I shall not return home yet. I shall follow up a venture with this child here. It may be my very last chance."

Henry waited for Prince Pollock to seat himself and then placed a knife in the prince's waiting hand. He did not look at Ketti, but she had the feeling he did not approve of her. "Very good, sire," was all he said. "I shall ready our belongings."

"You will not be coming with me."

At the prince's words, Henry's eyes slid to take in Ketti. "Is that wise, sire?"

" 'Tis wise, 'tis wonderful!" Prince Pollock said giddily. "While I am gone, you must inform my brother that I am embarked on a dangerous mission to rescue a princess and that I have been especially sought out." The prince looked to Ketti for confirmation, and she nodded vigorously. "When do we leave?" he asked her.

"Right away. My friend is waiting for us at the city's north gate."

Standing stiffly at the prince's side, Henry inquired, "Is this friend of yours someone who can care for his royal highness?"

Ketti bit her lip, thinking. She didn't want to say anything that might ruin her plans. "I guess. He was a coachman once."

"There you are," said Prince Pollock. "A servant. I will be well taken care of, Henry, so stop being such a worry-wizard." He stood, and his breakfast tumbled to the floor. Henry dropped to his knees to mop up the mess.

"Very good, sire. I will see to it that your horses are saddled."

The two horses brought to the front of the Thirsty Mug were decked out in bell-studded harnesses. Both wore draperies, one piece skirting their rumps and another covering their heads and hanging almost to the ground. A proud-looking white horse had the more elaborate costume, its saddle gilded and set with pearls, but Ketti's heart went out to a quiet and smaller brown horse. When she circled the horse's neck with her arms, he nibbled her with velvet lips.

"May I ride this one?" she asked.

"Certainly not!" was the muffled answer.

Prince Pollock was no longer recognizable. He was dressed in a helmet and a chain-mail hauberk that went from his shoulders to his knees. A sword in a scabbard dangled low on one hip.

"That horse is Traveler, and he is my palfrey," the prince said as the servant Henry steered him forward.

"What's a palfrey?" Ketti asked. She watched the prince climb awkwardly onto the brown horse's saddle, using Henry's clasped hands as a step.

"It's the horse I ride when I'm not in battle," he called down. "In battle, I ride Blanchart, my war-horse, whom you may have the honor of leading."

"Leading?" Ketti said. "You mean I don't get to ride?"

"It would not be proper."

Prince Pollock clicked his tongue to get Traveler started. Reminding herself to be grateful for any prince at all, Ketti took the white horse's lead from Henry's hand and started forward. Both horses followed her down the lane, and the air was instantly filled with the jingling of their harness bells.

"How will I recognize your friend?" shouted Prince Pollock.

"What?"

"I said, how will I—"

Ketti could hardly hear over the ringing of the bells. "This is ridiculous," she complained.

"Yes," she thought she heard the prince answer. "We do look good, don't we?"

"What?" she asked. "We've got to get rid of the bells!"

"Thank you," the prince replied. "I had it made when I was knighted!"

The streets of the city seemed busier than ever. Instead of buying and selling, people were calling and running. Even if they took an interest in the prince and his horses, they quickly turned back to whatever frantic business was at hand. The farther Ketti walked, the more worried she became. Would anything stop her from getting out of the city?

"There it is," she announced with relief when she'd caught sight of the gate.

"No, thank you, I'm not hungry," Prince Pollock replied through the jangling bells.

Annoyed, Ketti prepared to repeat her words more loudly. But before she could, a gloved hand with a viselike grip came down on her arm.

"Halt!" a broad soldier in a red uniform told her. "You'll follow at once. It is commanded."

Blanchart reared in fear, and his lead slipped out of Ketti's grasp.

"Unhand my steed!" Ketti heard Prince Pollock order as he was surrounded by a troop of soldiers. "Take the child if you must, but unhand my—*Ooof!*" Dragged backward off Traveler, the prince was quickly silenced.

Ketti tried to fight, but the soldier was much

stronger. He moved her along the lane as easily as a man might pass a saltcellar down the length of a table. All too soon, it became apparent that he was taking her to the castle. But why?

Ketti imagined a list of reasons, and none of them were good—the king was angry she had slipped a soldier in to take a prince's place, the cold-hearted princesses had discovered her part in their downfall, the soldier had revealed the magic cloak and Ketti was wanted as a witch. Were witches executed as quickly as failed princes? Were the people gathering in the square for another show?

With Ketti struggling against her captor, the portcullis lifted before her, gears grinding. Shoved forward, Ketti had just time enough to glimpse the grinning porter's pockmarked face before she was plunged into the murky shadow of the donjon.

The fortified tower dwarfed everything. At least a hundred feet across and twice as high, it seemed built for a race of giants. Its curving wall was broken only occasionally by windows, much too high to be entered by an enemy. Its far-off top was girdled with sharp triangles of stone.

"Move along," the soldier growled.

He shoved Ketti into a narrow and gloomy space within the donjon that was filled with musty air and the echoes of voices and boots slapping against stone. On both sides of her were stairs, spiraling up and down with the curve of the outer wall. Donjon, donjon . . . dungeon! With the connection, Ketti's mind conjured a vision of underground cells so real she could almost feel the manacles on her wrists. When she heard a friendly voice speak above her, she broke away from her captor and began climbing the oversized stairs.

"Little one," the voice came again. "Do not be afraid!"

Ketti found the kind soldier on the level above the entrance. He was dressed entirely in garments made from gold cloth. Humor glinted in his eyes as he asked, "Will you miss my green uniform?"

Ketti had been so terrified that she burrowed her face in his chest and sobbed with relief. He stroked her hair and tried to soothe her.

"There, there. I'm sorry you were frightened. I should have realized the soldiers would not be gentle with you. When I am king, I shall put order into their ranks. But come now and let me tell you how it went for me."

Passing through an arched doorway, he led her into a cavernous room that featured both a hole in its vaulted ceiling and a hole in its floor. The room was bright with sunlight, since the donjon's distant roof was open to the sky.

"I did everything as you instructed," the soldier began.

He told Ketti how he had been settled in a room beside the princesses' bedroom and how he'd avoided drinking the drugged wine by pouring it into a sponge hidden beneath his beard. When the princesses had believed him to be asleep, the eldest one had knocked on a bed, which then sank into the ground. As she and her sisters had descended, the kind soldier had thrown the hooded cloak over himself and followed.

"Underground," he told Ketti, "there were avenues of wondrous trees. The first had leaves of silver; the second had leaves of gold; and the third had leaves made of diamonds."

He went on to tell Ketti how the princesses had been rowed in boats across a lake by twelve young men who had then escorted them to an underground castle.

"There they danced until their shoes were worn out," he finished.

When he clapped his hands, a servant appeared carrying a platter. On it lay three twigs, one from each of the trees, and a jewel-encrusted wine cup.

"These I took on the third night," the kind soldier explained. "This morning, when I answered the king's question, I produced all these tokens to show I had spoken the truth. In gratitude, I give them to you. May they be of some value to you, and may they make up for my blunder. You see, I cannot return your fine cloak. After speaking to the king, I went back to my room and discovered that the cloak had disappeared. It is another mystery to be solved, although I have my suspicions and shall keep close watch on my wife-to-be and her sisters."

Ketti felt sorry when she thought of the soldier's

future life. When she had read the princesses' story, she'd thought only of their beauty. She'd even imagined herself as the youngest, the one who became frightened when the soldier snapped off the twigs and stepped on her gown. Now, vaguely ashamed, Ketti saw that the sisters cared only for their own happiness, even at the expense of others.

"The wedding is to be celebrated today," the soldier said. "Since I am no longer young, I have chosen to wed the eldest princess. The orders have already gone out for our feast. Even now, an announcement is being made in the square."

So that was what the fuss had been about, Ketti realized.

"Before I show myself to the crowd," he said, "is there anything I can do to help you?"

Ketti knew exactly what she wanted. "Could someone take the bells off Prince Pollock's horses? It's important that we don't attract attention."

"Say no more," the soldier said. He sent the servant away to do as Ketti had requested. "May you journey in safety, little one. May you find your heart's desire."

"How did you know?"

The soldier touched her hand. "It is what we all seek, little one. Some find it, some find something else."

When Ketti was reunited with Prince Pollock and the rat outside the north city gate, she found the prince in an uproar.

"My harnesses have been mutilated! And now this disgusting creature speaks to me and demands that you ride my palfrey!"

"Time works against us!" the rat shouted.

Ketti hooked a drawstring pouch containing the twigs and the wine cup onto Traveler's saddle. She had to stretch her leg up very high to reach the stirrup.

"He's right," she told the prince. "You've got to kiss Briar Rose before the full moon or you'll go back to your brother empty-handed."

Seeing Prince Pollock frown, Ketti worried he would change his mind about going. But when he spoke, it was of another matter entirely.

"You promised me a servant, Ketti Watson. I cannot mount Blanchart unassisted."

"Step onto a rock," the rat said without sympathy. "There will be time enough for pampering after you've woken Briar Rose and we've gotten our happily-ever-afters."

Although Prince Pollock did as he was told, he was clearly displeased at being ordered about.

"Coachman, eh?" he muttered. "He will be more of a footman, now. I still have some rights, and I will not have my steeds ridden by a rodent!"

# CHAPTER 9

# *Across the Sweep*

The day was sunny as they set out. The rat led the way past recently harvested fields and quaint cottages, over gentle hills and through bare but friendly woods. By midafternoon, though, the sky paled, seeming to pull back and abandon them. As they reached a steep slope, a wind sprang up—damp, heavy, and smelling of earth.

"Do we have to go this way?" Ketti asked.

The horses were struggling to follow the rat up the slope. Their hooves slipped on loose dirt and stones.

"It's the only way to reach the Sweep," the rat told her. He was breathless from the climb, and Ketti turned to the prince for an explanation.

"What's the Sweep?"

Prince Pollock had lost his helmet at the start of the slope. With his arms flung around Blanchart's neck, he attempted an offhand answer through gritted teeth.

"It's nothing, nothing except something to avoid. Don't worry. We're sure to go around it."

Ketti nodded without understanding. Was it water they had to skirt? Then why call it "nothing"?

At the top, Ketti looked around and thought immediately of the ocean. On her face was a mist of water, her ears hummed with a low rushing sound, and before her eyes lay wave after wave after wave. But it wasn't the ocean. It was the Sweep, a rolling, brown, seemingly endless stretch of land.

Prince Pollock shouted to be heard over the wind's moaning. "WE GO AROUND IT, OF COURSE!"

"WHAT, AND WASTE TIME?" the rat snapped. "WE GO ACROSS IT, OF NECESSITY."

When the rat plunged forward, Ketti squeezed Traveler with her knees, encouraging him to follow. Behind her, Prince Pollock voiced a protest, but Ketti couldn't make out his words and didn't try to. The Sweep looked all right to her. True, there weren't any trees to shelter them; there was nothing but low-growing, sad-looking, scrubby plants. And there was the wind against them. But what was wind, what was moisture? Ahead, perhaps five miles away on the horizon, she could see a wood. Just beyond it, she knew, were both Cinderella's palace and the sleeping castle. Beyond the Sweep lay happily-ever-after.

At first they kept to the crests of the hills, where the ground was rocky. When their way was barred by boulders, they were always able to sidestep them with a little backtracking. But then the mist became a light rain and the horses began to lose their footing on the wet rocks.

Prince Pollock dismounted and had Ketti do the same. "THE HORSES WILL BREAK THEIR LEGS IF WE'RE NOT CAREFUL," he shouted, adding, "CURSE THIS AWFUL WIND!"

Progress slowed. For every hill that was left behind, another rose up in the distance. The wood Ketti had thought she'd seen was always ahead of them, never allowing itself to be reached. Finally, when a path they had been following twisted and narrowed and brought them straight up to a jutting crag impassable for all except the rat, the vote was unanimous: They would descend to the low ground.

"LOOK!" Ketti said, pointing, as they picked their way downward.

Above, wings outstretched, was a bird, black like the one that had flown out of the silver linden tree. Rising and dropping on air currents like a glossy black kite, it seemed to mock their clumsy efforts.

Ketti started, "Do you think—"

"Don't think," the rat commanded her. "Walk."

The lower ground was soggy. Instead of boulders, there were streams to block them. Although the shallow ones could be crossed, they had to navigate around the deeper ones.

"It's okay, it's okay," Ketti murmured, trying to soothe Traveler. Feeling the suck of mud beneath him, the horse pulled back nervously on his lead. Ketti aimed him at the tufts of grass and reeds and found that their feet sank nonetheless. Water oozed into her sneakers. Prince Pollock was having a tougher time of it. With each gust of wind, Blanchart alternately reared and pawed the ground, his nostrils flaring in terror. No one mentioned the bleached bones and skulls that were littered about, remains of unlucky sheep and cattle that had been lost in the marshes.

"THIS WON'T DO," Prince Pollock hollered ahead to the rat as yet another stream blocked their way. "WE'VE BEEN GOING AROUND SO MUCH THAT WE'RE BACK WHERE WE CAME UP THE SLOPE!"

Was it true? Everything looked so much the same to Ketti that it was hard to tell. Drenched and thinking of the bones, she shivered.

"WE'LL HAVE TO GO UP AGAIN," the rat called, "OR ELSE GIVE IT UP FOR TODAY AND CAMP."

"WE COULD DO WITH A REST," Prince Pollock agreed.

In the rain, in the wind? They might camp, Ketti thought, but they wouldn't rest.

"THIS WAY," the rat shouted, jerking his muzzle up, "WHERE WE WON'T BE FLOODED OUT."

It was in scrambling to higher ground that they saw her. She stood atop a pile of rocks crowning a distant hill, with the tattered ends of her dress flying in the wind and a broom raised above her head. There was no mistaking who it was.

"HADUWIG'S HERE!" Ketti screamed. "SHE SEES US!"

Mesmerized, they watched the witch wheel her broom around and around. Thunder boomed, lightning sparked. Then black clouds danced in a circle overhead and burst, spilling instant desolation.

"I CAN'T SEE!" Ketti screeched. Frantic, she spun around, trying to peer through the downpour, fearful the witch would come up beside her at any moment.

"MOUNT!" she heard Prince Pollock order. "WE'LL GIVE THE HORSES THEIR HEADS. THEY DON'T WANT TO BE NEAR THAT CREATURE ANY MORE THAN WE DO!"

Although the rain was blinding, Ketti was close enough to see the prince scoop the rat off the ground before he struggled onto a rock and then up onto Blanchart's back. After pulling herself onto Traveler, Ketti huddled over his saddle and hoped with all her might that Prince Pollock's faith in the horses would be justified.

For a full hour, they plodded through the driving rain. Although the horses slid and sank and stumbled, they kept on until, with the arrival of darkness, the rain let up.

The sudden quiet was eerie, the only sound the ominous hissing of swollen streams. Ketti found herself remembering Prince Pollock's earlier description of the Sweep: nothing. That was it exactly. They were wandering in a black, vast nothing.

When the moon appeared, it was softened by a

milky haze and ringed by a halo of white light. Just beyond half, it looked waterlogged to Ketti. But then, she thought, everything looked waterlogged to her. She was sitting on a soggy saddle in dripping clothes, riding a wet horse that was cloaked in drenched draperies.

"We've got to stop," she heard the prince whisper. "The horses are foundering. Do you think we've outrun her?"

The answer came in a flash of red eyes. Ketti screamed as Traveler reared. Off balance, she reached for something to stop her fall and only succeeded in pulling away the drawstring pouch that held the kind soldier's gifts. With a thud, she landed on the ground and stared up at the witch's grinning face.

"Such a helpful girl," the witch crooned.

Ketti dragged herself backward through the mud. Above her, Haduwig's nails flashed menacingly as she stirred the night air with her broom.

"Helping the rat—*uoypots*—helping the prince— *uoypeels*—helping dear Briar Rose—*uoyeid*—and now you shall help me."

Ketti tried to inch away as the witch spoke, but somehow the broom remained always just above her head.

"You won't find me ungrateful," the witch promised.

Her voice was like a salve, thick and smothering. Ketti found movement more and more difficult.

"I shall grant you a painless death—*uoypots*. It will be like falling asleep—"

Weaker and weaker, Ketti stared into Haduwig's fiery eyes and knew escape was impossible. She groped on the ground around her for something to throw at the witch. A rock aimed just right, a sharp stick . . .

"—and if you suffer dreams of darkness—*uoypeels*—"

Ketti's fingers closed around mud.

"—endless dreams of shadows and confusion—*uoyeid*—you mustn't blame me—"

The pouch had opened, spilling two of the twigs onto the ground. In desperation, Ketti picked them up and hurled one through the darkness.

"—because I wish you no harm," the witch was saying.

Ketti's effort was a feeble one, and the twig fell short of its goal. Without a sound, it dropped to the earth, stem-side down.

"It was not I who encouraged your interference—*uoypots*." The broom went around and around. "You have bought your own doom. You see that—*uoypeels*—don't you? You must die now—*uoyeid*. First you, next the rat, and last the prince."

But something was happening. Ketti felt her feet shake. Something was springing up from the earth. A wall was growing between her and Haduwig, a shining, silver wall: a tree.

In the time that it took the witch to shout "*ESRUCUOY!*" Ketti, the rat, Prince Pollock, and the horses were encircled by a grove of silver trees. In a maddened rush of growth, roots spread, branches intertwined, and leaves lapped one over the other.

"*ESRUC*—"

There was sudden silence as the trees met overhead.

"What is this? Who was that?" Prince Pollock swiveled his head to take everything in, then moved to the spot where Ketti lay. Bending awkwardly in his hauberk, he asked, "Are you all right?"

Ketti tried to answer but her mouth would not cooperate. She could not speak; she could not sit up. She could not, in fact, command her body to do anything at all.

"The witch's spell," she heard the rat say. She felt his smooth pink paws take hold of her right index finger and jiggle it, as if to bring back life. Then he moved on to her middle finger, her ring finger, her pinky. In, out, in, out, up, down, up, down.

While he worked, the rat told Prince Pollock about Haduwig. Trying to be helpful, the prince patted Ketti's legs. She felt the same dull heaviness she'd experienced in the dentist's chair, when she'd been numbed with Novocain. But then just half her lower lip had been affected. Now it was her entire body.

"Pollock, look at this," the rat said when he'd gone around to Ketti's left hand.

Ketti tried to think. There was something in her hand, wasn't there? She took her mind down her left arm and traced her fingers. Yes, her fingers were curved, they were squeezing an object. But what? Something hard and shiny: a twig.

"The thing's glowing!" Prince Pollock said. "And—ow!—it's hot! We had better get it out of her hand before it burns her!"

Ketti's fingers were pried loose. When the twig was gone, her hand throbbed with warmth.

"Drop it, Pollock!" the rat said excitedly. "It's flaming up!"

Golden light flickered on the leaves above Ketti. The rat spoke in her ear.

"You had a little branch in your hand. It looks as if it's made of gold. It's burning now. It's making everything dry and warm."

"May they be of some value to you," the kind soldier had said. The silver and the gold twigs were helping her. One had saved her from the witch, the other was giving comfort. But what about the wine cup and the diamond twig? Were they safe? Ketti strained to look for them and couldn't budge. Beside her, the rat was whispering again.

"Try to relax. Perhaps the witch's spell will lose its hold on you."

Shadows swelled and shrank around Ketti as the horses were tended and things were spread out to dry. Not able to relax, she took inventory. She could swallow, she could—yes, she could open and close her eyes if she concentrated very hard. Her hand was pulsing, and she knew when someone touched her even if the feeling was strange and dull.

"Sleep now," the rat said, breaking into her thoughts. He patted her cheek with his forepaw. "Sleep."

At the tender touch, a sob escaped Ketti's throat and tears burned her eyes. They overflowed the corners to trickle down her nose and run into her ears, and she couldn't lift a hand to wipe them away.

Except for a distant gurgle of running water, all was still once the prince and the rat had settled themselves for the night. Then Prince Pollock started snoring and the horses dropped to the ground, shifting heavily until they were comfortable. But Ketti wasn't ready to sleep. Sleep was what Haduwig had intended for her, sleep with no waking, and the witch had come much too close to completing the spell. Could it ever be undone?

"—and we'll prop her up," the rat was saying when Ketti woke.

"You don't think she'll fall, do you?" Prince Pollock asked.

"Our other option is to lay her across the saddle, which would be far less comfortable."

Slowly, Ketti eased her eyes open. The space under the silver trees was filled with a shimmering white light. She blinked uncomfortably a few times and was relieved when Prince Pollock appeared above her to block the glare.

"She's awake," he said. "Now listen, Ketti. We're going to wrap you up in Traveler's draperies and attach you to his saddle."

"First see if she can move," the rat suggested. "Maybe she's better today. Did you see how she rumpled her face at the light? You can move, Ketti, can't you?"

Of course she could, Ketti thought. First she would smile. Then she would pull herself up until she was leaning on her elbows, just to be sure she wasn't dizzy, and then she would stand. She would. If she could only remember how!

"She's not doing anything," Prince Pollock observed. "Let's get her wrapped up. For all we know, that Haduwig creature is just outside the trees. When we break through, we had better be ready to ride."

As if swaddling a helpless infant, Prince Pollock bound Ketti in one set of draperies and tore up the other to secure her to the horse. After poking her gently, to be sure she would not easily tip to one side or the other, he turned and surveyed the sheltered circle of ground. The gold twig had burned itself out, but the drawstring pouch, holding the wine cup and the diamond twig, lay just where they had fallen from Traveler's saddle.

"What's this?" Prince Pollock asked as he reached inside.

The diamond twig emerged from the bag fizzing and sparking. At once the silver trees began to dissolve.

"Mount, mount!" Prince Pollock cried.

The next moment was one of utter confusion. The prince dropped both pouch and twig to hurry to Blanchart. Then he raced back, retrieved the pouch, and looped it onto Traveler's saddle. Meanwhile, the rat rushed around the diamond twig, shouting, "Is it hot? I don't think it's hot. We mustn't leave it here. Pick it up, pick it up!"

Since Ketti could do nothing but watch, it was she who saw the last traces of silver evaporate into a dull pewter sky. It was she who saw the black figure rise up from the side of the hill to nod and smile. Ketti strained to warn the others, but the most she could do was shift her eyes violently from the rat to the witch to the prince and back to the witch again.

Prince Pollock hurriedly placed the rat in front of Ketti.

"More witch work!" the rat warned, seeing Haduwig raise her broom.

As the prince pinched the diamond twig between two fingers and struggled onto Blanchart, a thin white stream of vapor emerged from the witch's broom. The vapor spread above them like milk spilling from a glass. And though the horses set off at a good pace, Haduwig's spell moved faster. Soon the entire sky above the Sweep was white. Heavier than the air, the white mist dropped in thick billows, sapping away color as hoarfrost grew, water froze, and plants withered.

Prince Pollock was grim. "We're doomed," he said as the vapor closed in around them. But when the prince put up the hand that held the diamond twig, the deadly fog curled back.

"They repel each other!" the rat shouted excitedly. "The diamond twig and the witch's spell repel each other!"

Had she been able, Ketti would have smiled. It was a miracle! They were protected from Haduwig's evil by an invisible force field. Unable to twist around and see the witch's reaction, Ketti watched the hills emerge from the mist, one after another, seemingly without end.

"Persevere," the rat encouraged her. "You seem better today, and we'll have help for you soon."

But as the day wore slowly on, Ketti found it increasingly difficult to stay awake. Lulled to sleep by the steady, rocking movement of the horse, she repeatedly woke in panic, gasping for air and convinced she had ceased breathing. Neither the rat's clucks of sympathy nor his pats of reassurance could ease her fright. It was all too clear that the witch's spell was not releasing its hold on her.

When the horses slipped down a slope at dusk, Ketti was hardly aware. It was like a dream when hands lifted her from Traveler and carried her into a palace. And by the time she was lowered into a warm bath, washed, and put to bed, she was lost to the world.

# ✳ CHAPTER 10 ✳

## Hearthside

The first thing Ketti became aware of was a dull pain throbbing in her left hand. Tucked into a strange bed, she pulled the hand out from beneath a fur cover and discovered someone had bandaged it.

"My sister will be relieved to hear you are awake," a woman on one side of the bed said. Her voice was unpleasantly flat, her face long and somber with oversized features.

"Sister was sure she had used the wand correctly," said a voice from the other side of the bed. Ketti turned to see a second woman, as homely as the first. "But then when you slept on and on . . ."

Ketti's right hand flew to where her hip pocket should have been, to where the wand should have been. But she was not wearing her own clothes. She was dressed in a kind of linen chemise.

"Where am I?" she asked. "Where's the wand, and who are you two?"

The room where Ketti found herself was chilly. Its stone walls were pierced by several arched windows that emitted the rosy glow of a sunrise or sunset.

"I'm Gert," said the first woman.

"I'm Gyth, and this is Hearthside," the second woman said. "The wand . . . well, I shall let Sister tell you. Are you well enough to join her now? Everyone will be at dinner in the great hall."

When Ketti nodded, Gert laid a red velvet gown onto the end of the bed, saying, "Sister said you should wear something of hers when you got up since your clothes were taken away to be washed. This should fit."

The dress before Ketti was loose and sleeveless, trimmed with ermine. Gyth laid beside it a smaller garment, something like a blouse with long, trailing sleeves, and a belt of woven cords. Ketti pushed back the fur cover to begin dressing, but the sudden movement left her hand aching. She drew it back to cradle it protectively.

"Your wound will take time to heal, I'm afraid," Gyth said.

Bunching up the gown, Gert lowered it over Ketti's head to help her dress. "Did you know it is three nights and three days since you arrived? The rat is beside himself."

Ketti carefully pushed her hands through the

armholes, calculating how much time was left before Briar Rose's spell ended. "But that means there are just two days left to reach the sleeping castle!"

"It's not the hundred-years spell that worries the rat," Gyth said. "It's you. He blames himself greatly for not rescuing you from the witch."

When the blouse was laced shut, Ketti moved off the bed. The gown added a graceful sweep to her every movement. She felt like a dancer—a princess!

Gyth observed her thoughtfully. "Our shoes would be too large for you, and Sister has an especially tiny foot. I hope your own shoes are dry."

"What odd ones they are," Gert added. "The rat tells us you are from a faraway place. How strange it must be there."

Ketti's shoes were dry. Wedging her feet into them, she discovered the sneakers were stiff and smelly, too. Following Gert and Gyth into a passage where torches smoked and flamed, Ketti no longer felt like a princess. She felt ready to trick-or-treat. And suddenly, as a draft of cool air rolled around her ankles, her mind cleared. Tiny foot. Was Sister Cinderella? Were the women before her the ugly stepsisters? What were they doing here? Why hadn't they been banished or beheaded?

Gert and Gyth led Ketti to a large, echoing hall inadequately warmed by an enormous fireplace. To Ketti, it had the appearance of a church, with a ribbed and vaulted ceiling, carved masonry, and beautiful windows of small colored-glass panes that formed pictures of knights and saints. There were four seated at the table: Prince Pollock, the rat, and a young couple. Every eye was on Ketti as she approached, and the only sound in the room was the crackling and popping of the wood fire.

Prince Pollock was the first to speak. "Awfully glad to see you up and about!"

"Very glad," the rat chimed in. After sending her a quick sharp-toothed grin, he said, "Ketti Watson, I'd like to introduce you first to Prince Edmund."

Ketti smiled shyly. This man looked like a prince to her, handsome and regal.

"You have already met Gert and Gyth," the rat went on, "and this is Princess Cinderella."

If all the others had crashed through the floor at that moment, Ketti wouldn't have noticed. Gazing at the fairy-tale princess, she forgot everything else. Cinderella was surely the most beautiful woman who had ever lived. There was sweet perfection in her face and expression. She moved across the floor toward Ketti to kiss her on the forehead.

"Welcome to Hearthside. I'm ashamed to say I did not recognize your friend the rat at first, but I am glad he remembered me. Now that I know how he was cheated, I will be pleased to aid him, and you as well."

"Sit and have some stag," Prince Edmund said.

Taking a place beside Prince Pollock, Ketti nodded, even though she wasn't sure what stag was. After a heaping plate had been placed before her, she still wasn't sure. Drenched with a pungent pepper sauce, the meat's flavor was elusive at best.

Prince Pollock poked fussily at his dinner. "Must we leave for the sleeping castle tonight, in the dark, with the witch out there?"

Ketti expected the rat to react harshly to the prince's seeming cowardice. His response surprised her.

"The morning will be soon enough."

"But the hundred-years spell," Ketti reminded him. "Aren't there only two days left?"

"You still need rest, and two days should give us enough time to reach Briar Rose." Seeing Ketti's unbelieving face, the rat explained softly, "I'm not about to put you in danger if I can help it, Ketti. When you were hurt by the witch's spell, I discovered something: I can't be happy if you aren't."

Where had she heard those words before? Of course—her father had said that if Ketti was unhappy then he and her mother were, too. Still, Ketti didn't really understand. She wanted happily-ever-after as much as ever.

"Tell her the good news," Prince Edmund urged.

"We're going with you," Cinderella said excitedly. "Edmund, myself, and our entire army!"

The remainder of the meal was merry, with talk about Briar Rose's awakening and Haduwig's inevitable defeat. As yawns grew frequent, though, the room emptied. First Prince Pollock and the rat left, then Gert and Gyth, and finally Prince Edmund, leaving Ketti alone with Cinderella.

The princess reached inside her sleeve and pulled out the wand. Ketti saw that it was wrapped, bandagelike, with white material.

"Did it break when I fell off my horse?" she asked anxiously. "Is there any magic left in it?"

"It is not broken," Cinderella said, "but whether it has magic left in it, I cannot say. You must understand that it was cut from the branch of a great silver linden tree many, many years ago, Ketti. The fairy godmother charged it with power by means of words I do not know. With each spell she cast, its magic lessened. I used it to counteract the spell the witch had placed on you. But instead of curing you instantly, it took you days to wake. I fear much of the wand's power is gone. If you are to use it with success, you must be sure that every possible advantage is on your side. For one thing, keep the wand wrapped until you need it."

Ketti nodded. That was easy enough.

"And wait to use it until its power is strongest."

"When will that be?"

"Its power will wax until the moon is full and then it will wane again."

"Wait," Ketti interrupted. "I get those two mixed up, wax and wane. Increase and decrease? The wand will be most powerful—"

"When the moon is full," Cinderella said. "It will also be more effective if the magic word is whispered."

"What word?"

As Cinderella passed the wand to Ketti, she said, "I cannot tell you. If the word is spoken, the wand will release a precious bit of its magic, and I do not believe there is any to spare."

"Then how can I use it?" Ketti asked desperately. "I want so much to be the best—"

Ketti broke off when Cinderella held out a piece of paper. Its edges were uneven, and it had been rolled up to the size of a crayon.

"The word," Cinderella said, "is written here."

Ketti swallowed. This was it. When she held the word and the wand together in her hand, she would also hold the means to happily-ever-after.

"Wait to read it until you are ready to cast the spell," Cinderella said. "Then think very hard about what it is you want. And Ketti," she added softly, "be sure you understand what you ask for."

That Cinderella, of all people, would question what she wanted was ridiculous, Ketti thought. "I only want the same thing you wanted, what you got—to be better than my sisters, to be special."

Cinderella shook her head. "But, Ketti, that wasn't my happily-ever-after. If I'm special now, I always was. The fairy godmother didn't change me. I didn't want to be better than my sisters. What I wanted was to be loved. And I am."

Lying on her side in the bedroom upstairs, Ketti was haunted by Cinderella's words. She stared out an arched window and saw the moon peeking back at her from behind a curtain of sky. Eyes, nose, and most of the mouth were visible. It was the same familiar face Ketti knew from home, but, for the first time, she found herself wondering what the face revealed. Were the white lips parted in surprise and wonder, or were they agape with horror?

Suddenly cold, Ketti snuggled deeper under the fur cover and closed her eyes to sleep.

# ✳ CHAPTER 11 ✳

# Black Feathers

"Obviously she has given up."

It was past midday. They had been riding through a bleak, gray forest since dawn, Prince Edmund beside Cinderella, Prince Pollock beside Ketti, the rat behind Edmund on a raised, flat portion of his ornate saddle, and the Hearthside army at their heels. The ground of the winding trail was hard, close to freezing, and the sound of the horses' hooves carried clear and sharp through the air.

"Haduwig realizes she cannot win and has retreated," Prince Edmund continued, his words puffing white in the chilly air. "That is why there has been no sign of her."

With a squeak of well-oiled leather, Prince Pollock shifted in his saddle to avoid hitting his head on the low branch of an oak. "It is because we are such an intimidating lot, eh, Ketti?" he asked.

Dressed in her own clothes, a bit stiffer from their washing, Ketti lifted the corners of her lips in a half-smile. Her hand, though scarred, felt better, soothed by the cold day. Still, Ketti found herself fighting off an uneasy dread, a dread she could trace to nothing more serious than the nip in the air and the ominous, mounting clouds above them.

"I almost wish she would show up," the rat said. "At least then we would know what she's up to."

"I tell you, she's up to nothing," Prince Edmund insisted.

Suddenly, the rat leaped to the ground to race ahead of the horses. "STOP! DO NOT APPROACH THAT ANIMAL!"

Plumped in the middle of the narrow trail ahead was the golden goose. To the shoe and odd collection of stones and grass already attached to the bird were added a bowl and a shuttle used for weaving.

Edmund put a hand to his sword. "What is that creature?"

After Ketti had explained about the golden goose, the princes dismounted to clear the path. Though they waved their arms and stomped their boots, the goose didn't budge. Finally Ketti slipped off Traveler, saying, "We'll have to think of something else."

Cinderella called, "If you get stuck to it, Ketti, I shall laugh and free you."

"But suppose you don't think it's funny?" the rat said. "We mustn't risk anyone getting stuck."

At Ketti's approach, the goose stood up on its webbed feet.

"What's the matter with you?" she asked the bird. "We can't go off the path here, there are too many brambles. You'll have to move."

"*Wooonk, wonk-wonk-wonk,*" the goose honked softly.

"Don't trust it," the rat warned.

Ketti nodded. "I know. I just can't get rid of the feeling that it understands what I'm saying."

She ran her fingers through her hair, thinking. Then she pulled the wrapped wand from her pocket. "Do you see this?" she asked the goose sternly. "Inside is a magic wand, and if you don't get out of the way, I'll magic you off someplace, far from here."

Instead of having the desired effect of bluffing the goose into retreat, the wand seemed to excite the bird. Unfolding its wings, it rushed at Ketti. Quickly the rat and the princes charged to their horses. Ketti ran, too, with the goose just behind her, breathing out a long hiss. It was nearly upon her when, on a hunch, she tossed the wand to Edmund. In its wrappings, the wand turned end over end, arching up, then falling neatly onto the center of his palm.

"Ride!" Ketti shouted.

With a kick to his horse's flank, Edmund took off down the track with the goose in close pursuit.

"That's strange," Ketti said as she remounted. "Why would the goose want the wand?"

Prince Pollock suggested, "Perhaps it is in league

with the witch and it wishes you to be without power."

"But once it saved me from Haduwig—"

"A ruse," Prince Pollock proclaimed, "to inspire your faith so that it might later trick you into giving up the wand."

With the army following them, they cantered forward, tracing the goose's path. The track narrowed and widened and narrowed again. It was a while before they met with Edmund. Breathless from a hard ride, he reported that the goose had grown tired and had dragged itself off into the brush.

"Another victory!" Prince Pollock exclaimed. "We have defeated not only the witch but her ally, too!"

Ketti couldn't share his buoyant mood. While the army sang ballads and the princes drank toasts, finishing the wine Edmund had brought as well as the remainder of the water, she worried. It seemed to her that the longer they evaded trouble, the greater the inevitable danger would be. A witch like Haduwig didn't nurse a grudge for a hundred years and then give up.

Yet nothing happened. The trail through the forest wound on without surprise, bringing them at dusk to an ice-sheeted pool.

"A good place to camp," Prince Edmund said. With his foot, he broke through to the water and let his horse drink. "We are more than halfway to the sleeping castle. Tomorrow will be an easy ride."

Cracking the ice in different places, the Hearthside

soldiers allowed their horses to drink and filled their waterskins. Ketti took on that task for Cinderella, the princes, and herself. Too thirsty to wait, Prince Pollock searched the drawstring pouch on Traveler's saddle for the jewel-encrusted cup and helped himself.

"Have some?" he asked, offering Ketti a fresh dip. It was then that the rat called out a warning for the second time that day.

"BLACK FEATHERS!"

"Where?" Ketti peered into the flawless vessel, seeing nothing but the cold, clear liquid.

"Here," the rat said, darting along the ground from one spot to the next. "Here and here. Rook feathers."

Prince Pollock was unconcerned. "So?"

"All day I have expected some action on the part of the witch," the rat said. "None has come, and now I understand why. Haduwig has hurried ahead to the sleeping castle in order to be in place when the full moon rises tomorrow night. But she has left evil work in her wake."

Prince Edmund looked bemused. "What evil work?"

"She has put a spell on the water."

At the rat's words, Prince Pollock swallowed and touched his fingers to his throat.

Prince Edmund took the waterskins from Ketti's hands. "You presume all this from the presence of a few feathers?"

"Rook feathers," the rat repeated. "From the rook that is Haduwig's spy and comrade."

"But . . . but I drank this water," Prince Pollock said in a halting voice.

"Yes, and you are fine." Prince Edmund shook his head defiantly and passed a waterskin to his wife. "Look around us. The horses have drunk from this pool and so has the entire army. If the witch has left any evil behind her, it is the legacy of fear."

As he had already done several times that day, Prince Edmund lifted a waterskin and proposed a toast. "To courage!"

Her eyes full of trust, Cinderella echoed, "To courage." Then both tipped back their heads and drank.

Ketti watched to see what effect the water would have. When there was none, she decided to drink, too.

"I shall drink before you," the rat said.

At his insistence, Ketti knelt and held the rim of the jeweled cup to the rat's muzzle. A minute later, he let out something like a laugh.

"I guess Prince Edmund is right! Haduwig's greatest legacy is fear. To courage!"

"To courage," Ketti said, downing the rest of the water.

As she lowered the cup, Prince Edmund's horse let out a grunt and fell to the ground. In nightmarish succession, the soldiers and the other horses followed.

"The water . . ." Prince Edmund's smile twisted out of recognition.

"It was bewitched!" Ketti cried. She watched Prince Edmund begin to move unsteadily toward the pool, cupping his hands together.

"I need more water," he said. "I shall die without it."

"I rather think you shall die with it," Prince Pollock replied. To keep Edmund from drinking, he seized one arm and ordered Ketti to take the other. But Cinderella and the army had turned back to the pond, too. Even the horses, wobbly but determined, were drinking more of the enchanted water.

"There aren't enough of us to stop them all!" Ketti wailed. She tugged without effect first on Edmund and then on Cinderella.

"That is why we must give it up," the rat said. "Let them drink. Come away, Pollock. Come away."

Ketti followed the rat to a large boulder, just out of sight of the pool. Within moments, Prince Pollock came after them, tears running down his face as he reported the news that Blanchart and Traveler were writhing on the ground in agony.

"It is a spiraling spell," the rat stated. "It relies on the inability of those who are stricken to free themselves from the circle of pain."

Ketti tried to understand. "The water makes them sick, which makes them want more water."

"Yes," the rat confirmed. "I don't imagine it needs much power, and I am reassured to think that Haduwig has resorted to it."

Prince Pollock wiped at his eyes indignantly. "Reassured?"

"If Haduwig had unlimited power at her disposal, she would have stopped us," the rat said.

"But she *has* stopped us!" Prince Pollock wailed.

The rat ignored him. "It is my guess that Haduwig's broom, like the godmother's wand, is emptying of power."

"That is good," Ketti said thoughtfully.

"Have you both gone mad?" Prince Pollock demanded. "Can you not hear the suffering?"

At that moment, several soldiers were howling with pain. Others groaned. The rat seemed not to notice any of it.

"Have either of you stopped to wonder something?" he asked.

"Yes. I wonder if you have lost all capacity for compassion!" Prince Pollock snapped.

Ketti's eyes were locked with the rat's. "Why aren't we sick?"

"I do feel unwell!" Prince Pollock said, putting a hand to his head.

Ketti answered her own question. "We all drank from the jeweled cup, the one the kind soldier gave me. Is that why we're okay? Do you suppose the cup would help the others?"

Without waiting for a response, Ketti ran back to the pool, where figures twisted like tortured ghosts drank and moaned and then drank again. The jeweled cup shimmered in the cold, white light of the newly risen and nearly round moon.

"Do not attempt to stop me!" warned a pale figure bent over the water. It was Cinderella, and Ketti could hardly believe she had ever thought the princess beautiful. At that moment, Cinderella's face was distorted as she snarled, "I must have more!"

After filling the cup, Ketti coaxed, "Try this."

Cinderella snatched the cup and drank. Instantly a change came over her face. She sank to the ground and whispered, "Thank you."

Next Ketti took the cup to Prince Edmund. After one sip, he, too, was sated.

"Pour some into the soldiers and the horses," the rat advised, joining Ketti. "Once they are calm, we will set up camp a distance from this cursed place."

Ketti did as she was told. When all who had been affected were bedded down around a series of campfires, she asked the rat, "Now what?"

"Everything will go on as planned," the rat told her. "Tomorrow morning we leave for the sleeping castle."

"But nobody from Hearthside is ready to travel," Ketti said. "The spell has left them very weak."

"Then we shall go alone on foot: you, me, and Prince Pollock."

Ketti reached back reluctantly to touch the wand in her rear pocket. "Do you think I should use magic to fix them up? It doesn't seem fair for them to suffer when they were only trying to help."

Beside her, the fairy-tale couple stirred.

"Dear Ketti," Cinderella said, "I should be very distressed to see you use the wand's last bit of power here. There is probably not enough left for all of us, in any event. We will recover. Your wine cup appears to have some power against spells."

"Take my sword," Prince Edmund said.

Since Edmund was too weak, Prince Pollock lifted the weapon for him, putting one hand on the gilt-adorned hilt and the other under the long, tapering blade. As he passed the sword to Ketti, Cinderella smiled.

"It will be twice as sharp as other swords, Ketti, because it is given with our love."

## ✳ CHAPTER 12 ✳

# The Sleeping Castle

On the last day of the hundred-years spell, Ketti, Prince Pollock, and the rat were up before dawn. By the time it was fully day, they saw the forest come to an end ahead of them. But to Prince Pollock's dismay, the trees did not give way to open land.

"There's a mountain to cross!"

The rat shrugged off his concern. "A mere hill," he said of the earth blocking them. "On the far side lies the country of the sleeping castle. Look upon this as our last hurdle."

Ketti's head tipped back to consider the task before them. For the first time in the adventure, she wished for a watch. How many hours would they spend climbing up, how many coming down? With the sun invisible in the cold and cloudy sky, there was no way to keep track of the shrinking time, no way to know if they would reach Briar Rose before moonrise.

In silence they climbed from ravines to tiny meadows sparkling with frost, from smooth sweeps of pale grass to rocky terraces. The frustrating part was that each feature concealed the one above it. Only occasionally did Ketti get glimpses of the hill's hazy summit. Twice, what she thought was the summit proved to be nothing more than one more ledge to cross.

Despite the cold, Prince Pollock stripped off his hauberk, finding it too cumbersome. Like Ketti, he went forth armed only with a sword hanging from a belt around his hips. When he spoke after a long silence, his words were spare and clipped with the effort of the climb.

"Sup at the top?"

"Dine on the downward incline," the rat answered.

Straining to pull herself up over a crag without putting pressure on her injured hand, Ketti was suddenly giddy. "Eat on the feet!" she piped.

"Champ and tramp!" the rat retorted and Ketti was sent into a nervous fit of laughter.

"March and munch!"

"Gulp and gallop!"

"Feed and—" Ketti's imagination failed her. They had crested the hill and any sense of achievement was dampened by the onset of icy rain.

"Feed and fall," Prince Pollock said glumly.

The whole valley was laid out before them, a

strange uneven patchwork of fields and fences. There was a disordered look to it all, as if plots had been staked out after endless squabbling. Houses were scattered here and there. Stone walls curved and angled, giving way to ragged hedges and split rails. Some boundaries had been made by old carts and broken tables, even by piles of garbage, forcing the roads linking one homestead to another to run mazelike throughout the valley. And smack in the center of all the confusion stood an enormous growing thing.

For a moment Ketti wondered what tree or bush grew in such a huge and shaggy fashion. Then she realized the rat had been wrong when he'd said the hill was the last hurdle. What they stared at were the thorns surrounding the sleeping castle.

"Drat," she said as Prince Pollock sucked in his breath.

The rat began the trip down, saying quietly, "The kingdom is a populated one."

Ketti hoped Prince Pollock didn't remember Roswald's dark prediction that there would be a fearsome fight should the king wake and demand that the squatters move off his land. She took out some of the food they had brought along and passed it around.

"You need loads of people to make a community," she chattered nervously. "Bakers and farmers and dressmakers . . . Think of all the taxes you'll be collecting!"

"Can you determine, from up here, the best route to the castle?" the rat asked. He, too, kept his voice light. Without Pollock there would be no prince to wake Briar Rose and no happily-ever-after.

"I think so," Ketti said. The sleet was falling steadily now. It was slushy beneath her feet. "I'm trying to remember a couple of landmarks. It won't be so easy to see the way when we're level with everything. Oh, but it won't be hard, either!" she added for Prince Pollock's benefit.

A left at the big brown barn, straight to the pasture surrounded by stones, right by the little green shed. Or was it first left by the house with the lopsided roof and then right by the little green shed? Darkened by rain clouds, the sky gave Ketti the feeling that the day was more done than not. The last thing they needed was to become lost on the twisting, rutted roads.

"Look at that!" she said with forced cheer. "I'll bet it didn't take half the time to get down that it took to get up the hill."

Ice was now forming on everything in sight, holding each blade of grass separate from every other. Ice grew thick on tree trunks, encased wheelbarrows and carts. It was beautiful to see, but it was also frightening. The ice seemed to distance them from the real world.

"Wrong way," she said as Prince Pollock moved to follow the road that angled around the corner of a cottage. "We make a left turn at the stile."

"Left?"

"Yes," Ketti insisted.

The rat shook his head. "I'm too low to the ground to know which of you is right, and we don't have time to be wrong."

"Let us ask for directions at this cottage," the prince suggested.

When he turned and faces pulled back from the windows, it occurred to Ketti that Haduwig was not the only one who might wish them to fail. Around them was a whole valley full of people risking eviction or at least taxation if the castle was wakened. Prince Pollock must have thought the same.

"Perhaps you are right," he said hurriedly. "Let us go your way."

Around the enchanted castle lay an empty corridor where no one had dared to settle. With a few more twists of the road, Ketti, the rat, and Prince Pollock stood gazing up at their goal. True to Gretel's word, thorns hid every feature. And every thorn, every stem, every branch was coated with a clear, thickening layer of ice.

The prince drew his sword. "Shall I have a go at it?"

"No," the rat said. "What good will it do if we hack at the thorns only to gain the blank face of the palisade? We must find the gate."

"We'll split up and look for a road," Ketti said, remembering King Birandell's city. "Prince Pollock, you go that way, and we'll go this way."

But what, she wondered as she set off with the rat, would a hundred-year-old road look like? Would it be hidden by windswept dirt, by generations of weeds? Using Prince Edmund's sword as a kind of walking stick, Ketti probed the ground with each step. Since the compound was large, spread over many acres, it was a long while before she and the rat had gone halfway around. Ketti was beginning to think that the road they sought had long ago disintegrated when she heard chopping. Rounding a corner, she saw the prince ahead of them with his feet set on the remains of an ancient cobbled path. He gripped his sword tightly in two hands, raising it over his head again and again to bring it down into the tangle of thorns.

"Let me help," Ketti said, arriving at his side.

The prince nodded without slowing his pace. "Pull the loose wood away."

Ketti did as she was asked. But the growth surrounding the castle was so thick that, even with the splintered branches moved, no dent was visible.

"I'll take over the chopping," she said when Prince Pollock paused to wipe his brow.

Ketti lifted Edmund's sword with two hands and grimaced as the weapon pressed the place where she'd been burned. When she lowered the sword with all her might, there was a sudden shattering of ice. All the thorny branches came tumbling down at once, to disappear as they touched the ground.

"You've broken the magic," the rat whispered.

Together they stared at a wall of stone. Too high to scramble over and topped with a fence of sharp stakes, it seemed at first to be yet another obstacle.

But tucked in the side of the wall was a wooden gate held ajar by a pile of clothes.

"Let's go!" the rat cried.

Ketti was the first to reach the fraying heap in the gateway, and she let out a strangled scream. The garments were not empty. A body lay loosely inside them, a man, gray skinned and white haired, eyes staring, mouth toothless, fingernails long and curved. All too vividly, he brought to Ketti's mind Prince Roswald's horrible claim that Briar Rose had gone on aging.

"The porter," was all the rat said, leaping over the man. "Come on."

Following, Ketti and Prince Pollock found themselves in an open space that was clogged with weeds. On its far side was a second wall and a second gate guarded by a sleeping squire, weathered but reassuringly young. A metal gong beside him was played softly by raindrops. When Ketti silenced it, running her fingers down its gleaming, wet edge, she heard something new: a soft, secret scurrying, like the scratching of a thousand quill pens on parchment.

"Rats," Prince Pollock hissed. "Let's keep moving."

The moat came next, a channel of black water barely crusted with ice and reeking of decay. On its opposite side was the bailey. There, trapped in time, soldiers slept over their dice, women, their hair ending in icicles, drooped beside a fountain dotted with rainfall, and children lay sprawled in a hundred-year-old game of tag. It was an eerie sight, made worse by the occasional flutterings of movement at the edges of Ketti's vision.

Rope, wax, soap—Ketti remembered the rat's tale of his desperate diet. In the sleeping castle, no rope, no thatched roof, no felt shoe was left unnotched.

On they pressed, past stables and barracks, by mews where birds of prey perched with hoods rotting atop their feathered heads, past shops where smiths and carpenters sat crumpled over rusting tools. A chapel, the cookhouse. Finally, beyond the door of the inner ward, they found the donjon and a massive stone palace.

"Look," Prince Pollock said. "The sky is clearing!"

Ketti stared off to the west, where the clouds had parted just enough to give a glimpse of the sun, large and red and low.

The rat's voice was hushed and urgent. "Our time is running out!"

Without another word, all three of them ran into the palace. They rushed by walls hung with antlers and scraps of tapestry. They raced beside long oak tables where heads nodded over mummified roasts. They hurried past a man lounging in a golden throne, then sped up a staircase.

"Which way now?" Prince Pollock shouted.

The rat's voice went high in panic. "I don't know!"

Intuitively, Ketti rushed to the end of the hall where another stairway spiraled into darkness. With her hand groping a wall gone slimy with mold, she shuffled up a series of crumbling stone steps. The prince and the rat came after her, their voices echoing off the curving wall in confusion.

"What do you see . . . do you see . . . see?"

For a time Ketti could make out nothing. "There's light above me," she said after a bit. "And something . . ." A pebble skipped down the steps behind her. "A spinning wheel?"

# ✳ CHAPTER 13 ✳
# The Final Spell

The room Ketti entered had tall, narrow windows marking each wall. High in a tower, it gave views of the valley in all directions.

"Here's what set off the spell," Ketti murmured, stretching her hand out to touch the spindle of a spinning wheel. Even after a hundred years, the point was needle-sharp. A drop of blood was beading up on her fingertip when Prince Pollock and the rat reached her.

The rat's concern made him cranky. "You are lucky the spell is too old to have an effect! That is just what we would have needed, you lying on the floor here, asleep for a hundred years . . ."

His talk of the floor led everyone's eyes to the pattern beneath the spinning wheel, an oddly shaped patch of clean floor amid the layers of dust. Here,

Ketti saw, had lain the head. Here an arm. Here a trailing dress. There was nothing now but a furrow stretching across the room.

"Someone has moved Briar Rose!" Prince Pollock exclaimed.

The trail of dust led to a dim corner where a huge, intricately carved, canopied bed stood. The curtains, the coverlet, and all the bedclothes had long ago been eaten away, but before them—perfectly pre- served, a blush of youth in her cheeks and a tiny smile on her lips—lay the princess Briar Rose, asleep.

"Poor child," the rat whispered lovingly. "Poor ill- starred child."

"Do it!" Ketti ordered Prince Pollock.

Through the west-facing window, she could see the sun. It was slipping through the sky like a raindrop down a windowpane.

"Kiss her!" Ketti insisted as the sun touched the far- distant trees.

Prince Pollock hovered beside Briar Rose's un- pillowed head. "I . . . I . . ." He looked at Ketti and shrugged. "I can't."

"What do you mean?!"

"She's so old," the prince began.

"Are you blind or only mad?" the rat demanded. "Briar Rose is beautiful! She outshines the sun, she puts the moon to shame!"

Through a window, Ketti could see the edge of the moon now. It peeped into a sky deepened to indigo.

"Briar Rose is one hundred and fifteen," Prince

Pollock whined. "I was wrong to come here. I could never marry a woman older than myself."

Ketti shoved the prince forward. "Wake her up! Think about Briar Rose, think about all those people asleep in the courtyard and palace! For once in your life, think about someone other than yourself!"

Shamed, the prince puckered his bulbous lips. Slowly he lowered his head. Closer, closer he came to the bed, to Briar Rose. Then, suddenly, his mouth fell open in a look of perfect horror.

"Something has my leg!"

"*UOYEID!*"

The awful, rasping voice filled Ketti's ears. Then something grabbed hold of her as well, reaching out from under the bed to wrap around her right ankle.

"So you thought you could beat me, did you?" the voice croaked. "First helpful, then clever, always lucky. But, my girl, all the luck in the world will not save you now!"

A quick tug by the witch sent both Ketti and Prince Pollock tumbling to the floor. Haduwig's fingers squeezed so hard that tears welled in Ketti's eyes.

"Oh, help," Prince Pollock whimpered as they were slowly drawn into the darkness pooled beneath the bed.

"Use your swords!" the rat shouted. "Ketti, the wand!"

The bed was so low that Ketti could not get to the wand in her back pocket. And when she drew Prince Edmund's sword, it was not long enough to reach the witch. On they slid. All Ketti could see were Haduwig's eyes, red and glowing. They pinned Ketti as though she were a bug on display. They seemed to know every wrong thing she had ever done, to know every rough shove to Ellen, every harsh word directed at Miranda. And those eyes approved.

"Yes, yes!" Haduwig began to laugh insanely. "I have waited long for this moment, Sister! You thought you could counter my spell, but it is I who have ruined yours!"

Suddenly Haduwig howled and let go. Ketti and Prince Pollock scrambled back into the room. The prince's face was drained of color, as pale as the moon escaping the horizon.

"Shall I kiss her now?" he asked.

Ketti nodded as a frightening figure emerged from under the bed. Long, sharp nails clutched a ragged broom, stick arms poked through tattered black sleeves, eyes burned from a skeletal head. And to one bone-thin leg clung the rat, his pointy teeth embedded in what little flesh hung there. While his bite had been enough to bring about the release of Ketti and the prince, it could not stop Haduwig completely.

"Kiss her now," the witch hissed mockingly. "Kiss her, if you can!"

Both Ketti and Prince Pollock raised their swords. But with supernatural strength, Haduwig swung her broom out and sent the weapons flying to the window.

"*Ebuoygorf!*" she shouted. Suddenly the prince was

no longer beside Ketti. In his place sat a frog with a thick, ugly head.

Haduwig's eyes rolled up to look toward something or someone only she could see. "It is I who has had the last say. With my last shred of power, Sister, I have defied you!"

Understanding flashed in Ketti's mind as the witch's perfect, white hands clawed the air between them: Haduwig was the fairy godmother's sister.

"And with my last ounce of life," the witch rasped at her, "I will finish you!"

Ketti fumbled to unwrap the wand as Haduwig hobbled forward, but the gesture was futile. There was not enough time. In desperation the rat filled the air with a harrowing scream, a plea for help. It was answered from a thousand places at once.

The soft, secret scurrying Ketti had heard earlier grew and grew until it was a thunderous march of feet. Like water bursting from a dam, rats leaped from the stairwell. One, three, twelve, fifty, a hundred. There were rats carpeting the floor and rats framing the bed. There were rats cascading over the spinning wheel and rats crowding the windowsills. They filled the room, tumbling one over another in their frenzy to get at the witch.

Ketti squeezed her eyes shut, unwilling to watch as the witch's form slowly shrank beneath a squirming, biting mass of rats. When she opened them again, the rats were leaving. They raced away with scraps of black rag, with bits of bone, with strands of hair, until there was nothing left on the floor but a frog and an old broom. Ketti breathed in a shuddering sigh as the room grew quiet.

"We failed," the rat said from beside Briar Rose.

Ketti twisted to look out the window. The moon lay cradled on the hillside. "It hasn't risen yet," she said. "There's still time. Kiss her!"

The rat gave a start. "What?"

"Kiss her, kiss Briar Rose!"

"I'm no prince!"

Ketti nodded rapidly, her certainty growing. "You are! The fairy godmother asked you to be, do you remember? She said, 'Be a prince,' and you were, to me. Maybe you weren't born a prince, but it's who you are inside. Oh, please, kiss her!"

Like a bird set free, the moon rose into the night sky. And the rat kissed Briar Rose.

In an instant, the girl on the bed opened her eyes and the furry creature Ketti had grown to love was replaced by a dark-haired man with large, kind eyes and a distinguished mustache.

"Happily-ever-after!" Ketti cried.

A change was coming over the castle. Laughter and song rang out, horses whinnied, falcons screeched.

"Briar Rose?" called a sleepy voice up the stairwell.

"It's Father," the princess said.

The man who entered the darkened tower room was the same one Ketti had seen asleep in the throne downstairs. He fell upon his daughter, showering her with tears and kisses.

"My darling, you're safe! Did it happen as the fairy godmother wished it? Have we truly slept for a hundred years?"

"A hundred years to the day," the rat-turned-prince acknowledged.

At his words, the king stood. "How can I thank you, sir? I do not even know your name."

Ketti thought back to when everything had begun, to the Kramer property and the game of hide-and-seek. "He's Humphrey Awl," she said. "Prince Humphrey Awl."

"You must not thank me," Prince Humphrey told the king. "You must thank Ketti Watson. Ketti is— how can I begin to list the good things about Ketti? She has a great desire to succeed and to see wrongs righted. Throughout our adventure, she has been clever and brave and resourceful. And now she must have her own happily-ever-after."

Ketti pulled the last of the wrappings from the wand. The sun was gone from the sky. The full moon had risen. There would never be a better time to use it. She had only to whisper the word and she would have her happily-ever-after. So what held her back?

"*Wooonk,*" came a sound as the golden goose waddled up the last of the steps into the tower room.

"How pretty!" Briar Rose said.

Prince Humphrey took the princess's small hand in his own. "Pretty to look at but not to touch."

The king, squinting, leaned forward to get a better view. "Why, the creature's made of gold!"

"Don't!" Ketti warned, but Briar Rose's father was already reaching to pat the bird on its head. Ketti thrust out her hand just in time to save him. But the sudden movement sent waves of pain through her wound. Her fingers opened, and the wand landed several feet away from her. The goose promptly dropped down on top of it. When the bird rose to its feet, tail wagging as merrily as a dog's, the wand was stuck to its golden feathers, a little to the right of the shoe, a little to the left of the shuttle.

"Your wand, Ketti," said the king as the goose toddled back down the tower steps. "Shall I order one of my men to fetch it back?"

The sword, the jeweled cup, the twigs, and the cloak—the magical help of those things had surprised Ketti. It was almost as if their power had come from the love with which they had been given rather than from the same kind of magic Haduwig had made with her broom, an evil magic meant to outdo a sister. Ketti wondered: Had the broom been cut from the same tree as the wand?

"No," she told the king. "No. It's all right. I've changed my mind. The goose knew all along what I had to learn—I don't want to be special by magic. Let the goose go."

# CHAPTER 14

# The Return to the Tree

When Cinderella and Prince Edmund arrived at the wakened castle with the horses, it was the shaggy and gaunt porter who announced them to the king. Standing in his baggy clothes, he asked leave to admit the royal couple, and Ketti learned he had been a wizened old man even long before his sleep.

"Please welcome all my new subjects as well," the king told the porter. "I shall want to meet each one."

At first the squatters came forth in twos and threes. But when news of the king's kindness spread, the numbers grew.

"It looks like your life will be happy from now on," Ketti told Prince Humphrey when she had a moment with him away from Briar Rose.

But Prince Humphrey wasn't smiling. "There is one

sadness that will remain with me amid all my joy, Ketti. I did not get you your happily-ever-after."

Ketti shook her head. "Maybe there is no happily-ever-after in my time."

"In your time?" Prince Humphrey's eyebrows shot up. "Oh my, yes! The wormhole! We've got to get you home!"

They were four on horses when they set off on the journey back to the silver linden tree. Ketti rode Traveler again, and Cinderella and Prince Edmund sat astride their mounts. But this time Prince Humphrey rode Blanchart, with Prince Pollock-turned-frog on the raised, flat portion of Edmund's saddle.

"Why not leave Pollock here?" Prince Edmund suggested on the last day, when they happened on a well near a castle. "Fresh water and lily pads. What more will he need?"

The frog that was Prince Pollock croaked, "But I can't swim!"

"We'll look in on you every once upon a time," Cinderella promised.

"And I'll let your manservant know what has befallen you," Prince Humphrey added.

Ketti had a flash of intuition. "You're 'The Frog Prince'!"

When the others looked blank, Ketti realized they couldn't have heard the story yet.

"Oh, what will become of me?" Prince Pollock asked anxiously as Edmund lowered him to the rim of the well.

Ketti smiled. "One thing is for sure—you won't have to worry about marrying anybody older than yourself. Watch for a girl with a golden ball—and teach yourself to swim!"

Sometime later, they rode into a meadow. When they reached the stump of a large tree, Prince Humphrey looked at Ketti in dismay.

"This is it," he said. "This is where the silver linden tree stood. But it's gone, chopped down, carried away!"

Ketti stared, unbelieving. "But that means I can't go home!"

Far up in the sky, a black bird turned slow circles. This had been Haduwig's last cruel act before rushing ahead to the sleeping castle, Ketti thought. Now there was nothing left. Every bit of the tree had been carried away. Ketti wondered if a piece of its wood lay on the woodpile behind her house. Did its struggle to return to its former self produce the effect of the wormhole?

"Come live with us," Cinderella told her. "Edmund and I would welcome you with love."

"Briar Rose and I also love you," Prince Humphrey said.

Ketti blinked back tears. The words she spoke came as a surprise to her, but once they were out, she knew the truth of them. "My own family loves me, too." Her mother and father couldn't be happy if she wasn't because they loved her. They loved her even though she was noisy and always in trouble. They loved her because she was Ketti. And maybe, just maybe, if she stopped acting like one of the twelve dancing princesses, thinking only about her own happiness, she could get along better with Miranda and Ellen. It wouldn't be easy. She'd have to swallow her pride sometimes, like Gretel had, and she'd probably fail every so often. But, oh, she wanted to try—if only she could get home!

"*Wonk, wonk, a-wonk!*"

"It is that cursed creature!" Prince Humphrey shouted. And before Ketti knew what was happening, both princes were chasing after the golden goose.

"Don't touch it!" she cried.

But Prince Humphrey tackled the bird with both arms. Prince Edmund piled on after him. Instantly they were glued to the bird and to each other.

"The wand will take you home," Prince Humphrey said through gritted teeth. Prince Edmund's chin was stuck to Humphrey's elbow. His knee was in Humphrey's side. "There is at least one bit of magic left in it. Show me the paper with the word on it, Ketti, and I will wish you home."

As he spoke, the princes struggled to raise themselves. But every move only made their predicament more ridiculous.

Cinderella wrung her hands, sobbing, "My darling, what will become of you?"

"I will be fine," Prince Edmund began. "The situation does not threaten my life."

"Perhaps we should consider sharing a castle," Prince Humphrey added as the goose swung its head and attached itself to his ear.

The idea of the princes bound together for life with the goose was so ridiculous that Ketti exploded with laughter. And all the pebbles and twigs, the little shoe, the shuttle, and the wand showered to the ground. Startled, Prince Edmund backed away, unbound, and Prince Humphrey opened his arms to let the goose go free.

"Did you laugh, too?" Ketti asked Cinderella.

The princess shook her head. Prince Humphrey said, "Don't you understand, Ketti? It was you. You are a princess."

Ketti laughed again. "I am not!"

"It's who you are inside. All this time you've been wishing to be special, and you already were."

Amazed, Ketti remembered what Prince Humphrey had told Briar Rose's father, that she was resourceful and clever and brave. But better than that, she was loved. Her happily-ever-after had been the same as Cinderella's, after all.

Beaming, Prince Humphrey picked up the wand and held it out to her. "The sun is gone from the sky. The moon, not quite full but full enough, is rising."

Ketti unrolled the scrap of paper to read what Cinderella had written. Was the word a wish or a state of being?

"Fare-thee-well," she whispered.

# ✳ CHAPTER 15 ✳

## Home Free All

There was no deafening silence, no blinding dark, merely a quick flash of blue light. One moment Ketti was staring lovingly at the faces of Prince Humphrey, Cinderella, and Prince Edmund. The next she was lying face down in the Watson flower bed, half hidden by a wild, fragrant growth of marigolds and geraniums.

"Home free all!" Miranda called, striding out into the yard. "The game's over. Mom wants us in for dinner, and I see you anyway, Ketti. You lose."

"You lose," Ellen echoed, appearing beside her sister.

Ketti jumped up and gave her sisters a quick hug. "I made it home and my hand is all better! I guess it was healed when the magic flowed out."

Miranda pulled back. "Magic?"

Seeing the doubting faces of her sisters, Ketti realized they couldn't understand what she was talking about. As far as they knew, she'd never been away. She'd arrived back home hours before she'd left.

"Never mind," she said, tucking the wand once more into her back pocket. "I was just making something up."

"What?" Ellen demanded. "Tell me."

"The true story of Sleeping Beauty," Ketti told her. "Did you know she was kissed by a rat?"

"*R* for rat," Ellen said.

"You have the best imagination, Ketti," Miranda added. "I could never think of the things that you do."

Ketti grinned with pleasure. "I know! Let's do my story as a puppet show. We can put it on for Ellen and Mom and Dad."

"Okay," Miranda agreed. "But you'll have to tell me what to say. We can use my old doll bed. After dinner."

"Right," Ketti said. But she didn't follow Miranda and Ellen to the house immediately. Instead she faced the back fence and looked toward the Kramer barn and the woodpile in front of it.

"Thanks," she said to the air.

Prince Humphrey and Briar Rose, Cinderella and Edmund, Prince Pollock, the kind soldier, the golden goose, Hansel and Gretel. She had known them. She had loved them. And they had loved her, long ago, once upon a time.